SECREꞮ ᴩOTION

Tony Flood

This edition is published by
Sportsworld Communications / Tony Flood
April 2018

best wishes

Tony Flood

SYNOPSIS

JODY, a bubbly 10-year-old girl with an unfortunate habit of saying the wrong thing at the wrong time, is desperate to find her missing brother James.

Her vivid dreams take her to a mysterious land called Tamila, which is inhabited by magical wizards, both good and bad, mischievous pixies, nasty witches and goblins and helpful fairies.

The unsuspecting girl falls foul of an evil wizard called Hugo Toby, who sends her into a whirlpool. But Wiffle, the wizard of kindness, arrives in the nick of time on his flying white horse to save her from drowning.

In her search for her brother, Jody has several hair-raising, terrifying – and sometimes hilarious – encounters. She has to battle against Hugo Toby and his vile brother Augustine The Awful, a cruel witch called Huffy Haggard, and two horrid goblins, all of whom are seeking the secret of everlasting life.

Jody also comes up against the most horrendous monster in the whole world. But she and her new friend, The Bag Man, who seems to have virtually everything in his carrier bags, are determined that good shall triumph over evil.

They refuse to give up despite having humiliating spells placed on them, with The Bag Man being turned into a frog!

REVIEWS

The Secret Potion contains so many weird and wonderful characters, including a frightful witch who places a nasty spell on poor Jody. It's a magical adventure for children and adults – and would make an excellent present, especially for Harry Potter fans.
– June Whitfield, actress and author.

Jody Richards is a MUST for everyone who wants to lose themselves in a thrilling adventure story. My children adored Enid Blyton and J.K. Rowling – and now they adore Tony Flood, too!
– Bill Smith, writer and parent.

I loved Jody dreaming herself into a magic land, but I feared for her safety as she tried to defy the evil forces and rescue her missing brother. The Secret Potion has everything – thrills, scares, delightfully crafted plots and great characters.
– Julia Sameja, mother, from Maidenhead, Berks.

The Secret Potion is a marvelous story – the wicked wizard Hugo Toby and his evil brother Augustine are just so mean – and I loved the double twist at the end!
– George Curtis, aged 15, from Hampton, Middlesex.

Reviews by author Jessica Duchen and journalist Chris Holmes are on the back cover.

ABOUT THE AUTHOR

TONY FLOOD has spent most of his working life as a sports and leisure journalist on various national and regional papers – but this is his first fantasy novel.

Tony, formerly Controller of Information at Sky Television, Editor of Football Monthly magazine and Sports Editor of the Lancashire Evening Telegraph, retired after eight years with The People newspaper. He is now content to write theatre reviews for the Brighton Argus and Eastbourne Herald.

His work as a leisure writer, critic and sports editor for the Richmond and Twickenham Times and Kentish Times Series saw him take on a variety of challenges – learning to dance with Strictly Come Dancing star Erin Boag, becoming a stand-up comedian and playing football with the late George Best and Bobby Moore.

Tony has interviewed some of the biggest names in the entertainment and sporting worlds – Muhammad Ali, Linda Gray, Britt Ekland, Frankie Howerd, Patsy Kensit, Petula Clark, Joe Pasquale, Seb Coe, Sir Alex Ferguson, Sir Bobby Charlton, Sir Bobby Robson and top comedy writers Galton and Simpson.

DEDICATIONS

THIS book is dedicated to the memory of my parents Mabel and Dennis Flood and my grandparents Winnie and Reggie Burwash, who brought me up with so much love and kindness.

They, together with my lovely wife Heather and son James, have been an inspiration to me as a writer.

Heather, who herself writes magical stories for young children, came up with the original idea for The Secret Potion, while James, a graphic designer, produced a superb book cover and illustrations for the first edition of this book. Now, in this second edition, designer Nicky Shearsby has provided a cover that perfectly projects the heroine Jody Richards and the horrific monster she faces.

I would also like to thank actress June Whitfield, author Michael Walsh and editors Jay Dixon, Lee Horton and John Payne for their encouragement and advice, as well as author Jessica Duchen, journalist Chris Holmes, Colin Downey, Angela and Sam Warren, Cathy and George Curtis, Julia Sameja and Bill Smith for their supportive reviews.

Special thanks go to Rex Sumner of My Voice Publishing for transferring the publishing rights to Tony Flood of Sportsworld Communications.

PROLOGUE

THUD, THUD, THUD. The sound of the door knocker woke Jody Richards from her night-time slumbers – and signalled that the police had arrived.

The sleepy 10-year-old girl sat up in bed with a jolt and glanced at her alarm clock – it was 9.25pm.

She listened from her bedroom as her mother Marjorie let two police officers into their smart semi-detached home in up-market Bromley before taking them into the spacious lounge where her father Herbert was sitting waiting.

Jody tiptoed downstairs into the hall and peered round the slightly opened lounge door as her parents exchanged pleasantries with the senior officer, Detective Inspector Ron Slater.

Slater, a tall man in his thirties whose expressionless, pockmarked face matched his dour character, reported that there was still no trace of Jody's missing elder brother James.

"But it's been weeks now since we reported him missing," Herbert protested. "Surely someone must have seen him." "Unfortunately not," replied the other policeman, DC Colin Browning, adjusting the designer glasses on his prominent nose.

"But on the law of averages, someone must know something," snapped Herbert. As an accountant, Jody's father knew all about odds.

"Nobody has answered our appeals, sir," said Slater. "James's disappearance has been covered in the Press and on television, and our colleagues have made house- to-house inquiries but they have produced nothing. Are you sure you and Mrs. Richards can think of no place your son might have gone? Or any reason why he might have run away? Perhaps there was something he was unhappy about?"

Jody wondered if the conversation had been cut short as an uncomfortable silence followed.

The suggestion that James had 'run away' and the inference that the Richards were perhaps in some way responsible was not picked up by Marjorie, a tubby women approaching her 40th birthday whose pleasant, freckled features were tense with worry.

Apart from her Women's Institute activities and her passion for clothes shopping, Marjorie's whole life was dedicated to her family. And Jody suspected that her mother was too shattered by James's disappearance to fully take in what was being said.

But the jibe was not lost on Herbert. "James was not unhappy and he has not run away, officer," he insisted, his anger and frustration telling in his voice.

"So you say, sir," the policeman replied. "But your daughter Jody told us James had confided in her that he wanted to go on an adventure holiday a few days before he disappeared. That suggests he may have run away.

"Did he mention to either you or Mrs. Richards anything about a particular place he would like to visit?" A holiday centre or a camping site, perhaps?"

"No," said Marjorie. "Nothing at all."

Jody could see her father begin to perspire and wipe his receding hairline. "We've already told you repeatedly, officer, we haven't a clue where James is," Herbert stressed. "But after being missing for three weeks, it's obvious that he has not run off. He's been abducted."

"Yes," added his wife. "Somebody must have kidnapped him."

"Usually, in such cases, a kidnapper would have demanded a ransom by now," said the pockmarked detective. "If he was abducted, I'm afraid money might not have been the motive."

"Please find him," pleaded a distraught Marjorie, bursting into tears.

Jody had heard enough. She was more convinced than ever that something dreadful had happened to her brother.

The determined, single-minded girl, whose Tomboyish behaviour caused her parents to shorten her full name of Joanne to Jo until she opted for Jody, believed it was time for her to take some form of action.

Should she go into the lounge and give the police details of the dream she had about James the previous night? And the visions she saw in her dream of a strange, mysterious land where he had gone?

No, they would scoff at her, just like her father had when she told her parents that she was old enough to take up skiing and bungee jumping.

At that moment Jody resolved that she would find James herself and end her mother's grief.

First, she would go back to bed and see if she could return to her amazingly vivid dream. It had been a lovely dream – revealing some dazzlingly beautiful sights and inhabitants – until she spotted a bad tempered man called Mr. Toby who frightened her so much she woke up shaking.

But her main memory was of a magical kingdom and a giant sign saying 'Welcome to Tamila'.

If she could dream about Tamila again she might even be able to find a way to follow her brother to this intriguing far off island.

CHAPTER ONE

SPLOSH! Jody's sandals and feet became soaked as she squelched her way through the wet undergrowth in the eerie, mysterious woods while the rain beat down on her. Her search for her missing brother James had somehow transported Jody from her cosy, warm little bedroom in peaceful Bromley, overlooking the Kent countryside, to the magical island of Tamila, amid exotic plants; rivers clean enough to drink from, and a blaze of colour.

Here trees and bushes were red and pink instead of the usual shades of green. They were every possible shape and size, some harmful and others harmless – matched in equal measures by the good and evil practised by the wizards, witches, pixies, goblins and fairies Jody had fleetingly seen in her dream.

There were no buildings in sight yet and she was starting to panic because she had no idea whether she was going in the right direction.

Even though it was clear daylight, the impulsive 10-year-old had got herself lost amongst a forest of towering trees and bushes with enormous pink leaves. They were so much larger than any she had seen before, and, when she tried to push past some of the giant leaves, they bounced back to hit her in the face.

'Just how did I get here?' Jody wondered. 'Did I dream myself here? But it can't be a dream – this is all so very real.' Certainly it seemed a bigger and more exciting adventure than those she had embarked upon previously in her young life.

Bigger than getting lost on the school journey to the Isle of Wight. And far more exciting than any of the 'dares' she had accepted from her school friends Gabrielle, Antonia and Grace – such as knocking a boy's hat off with a snowball or treading on a weighing machine being used by a bossy female teacher to make the women's weight appear to increase by an extra stone!

A sudden shower of rain left Jody's dress drenched because the rain drops – all bright red – were ten times as big as any she had ever seen before!

Quickening her pace, a relieved Jody eventually found herself in a clearing in which there was a large cottage. It's thatched roof and grey stone walls were rather grim and uninviting – in marked contrast to the brightly-painted cottages in the village nearby which she could now see in the far distance.

But Jody was so wet that she did not think twice about knocking on the large oak door, painted a more up-beat yellow.

After a few seconds it was thrown open and, to her horror, standing before her was the frightening figure of an overweight Mr. Hugo Toby, dressed in a black robe and resting on a walking stick

"What do you want?" boomed the nasty man, rubbing his pot-belly, which flopped over his belt, as he looked down at her with mean, uncaring, penetrating eyes under black, bushy eyebrows. He was unfortunate enough to also have a very long nose, but his chosen additions – wide side- burns and a small black beard – did nothing to improve his appearance.

Jody had dreamed about Tamila and some of its strange inhabitants only the previous night, including this intimidating fellow now confronting her. He had been the worst by far and had threatened to turn an otherwise pleasant dream into a nightmare.

Her appealing blue eyes were open even wider than normal with shock, but the startled girl knew she must resist the temptation to shout "It's you," and for once she did not make her usual mistake of saying the wrong thing at the wrong time.

Indeed, she struggled to find any words to answer this simple question because she was so consumed with dread by the evil aura that Mr. Toby portrayed.

She hardly noticed his protruding nose and goatee beard – instead her gaze was riveted to his large eyes, which showed an unmistakable glint of malice. 'He's probably a wizard,' she thought. 'Surely he's too big to be a goblin or a pixie.'

"Well?" he demanded. "Cat got your tongue has it?" He was actually referring to a large black cat, which had followed him out of his lounge. The cat, like his master, looked at the girl with disdain.

"I'm sorry to bother you, but I'm lost and wet," Jody finally told him, nervously stroking her soft golden-brown shoulder-length hair, causing some of the water to drain from it.

A few drops splashed on to Mr Toby, who glared at her disdainfully. Jody got the feeling that the sight of a young girl on his doorstep was undesirable enough, but one who splashed him with water was too much for him to tolerate! "Where are you looking for?" he said, still leaving Jody standing shivering outside as a gust of wind caused the rain to lash into her face.

"I don't really know," she stammered. "I am trying to find my brother James. He is missing from home and I think he's come here."

"And do you know whereabouts in Tamila he is?" asked Mr. Toby, rubbing his black beard impatiently.

"I'm not sure, but perhaps he is by the river – he loves to go swimming and fishing," Jody volunteered.

"The only river here leads to the whirlpool. Is that where you want to be?" Mr Toby bellowed above the sound of the wind and rain.

"Yes, that may be it," said Jody, hard pressed to prevent herself giggling as a raindrop fell on Mr. Toby's long nose. "You'd have to make your way through some dense forest and swamps to get to the whirlpool," he told her. "I don't think you'd have the stomach for it."

Jody was not familiar with the phrase Mr. Toby had used. Her eyes wandered to his ample midriff and, as he chuckled, his belly wobbled like a large jelly.

Before she could stop herself Jody said: "My stomach may not be as big as yours, sir, but I am determined to reach the whirlpool." The words were out of her mouth before she could stop them.

'Oh, dear,' she thought. 'I shouldn't have said that. Father's always telling me to think before I speak because I have a habit of saying the wrong thing. Hopefully, this gentleman will take it as a joke.' So she forced a smile.

Mr. Toby was not amused, however, and her smile was met with a scowl. "You are an extremely rude little girl," he admonished. "And it is hardly wise to insult a wizard."

"I'm sorry, sir. I didn't mean to offend you," she said through
chattering teeth.

Her face went bright red with embarrassment and the small beauty spot on her left cheek began to itch as it always did when she felt threatened.

"No matter – your wish is granted," roared Mr. Toby, snapping his fingers.

Suddenly Jody found herself lifted in the air and spinning through space before landing, with a loud splash, in the middle of a huge whirlpool.

She had no time for the shock to sink in because she was forced to fight to keep her head above water. But her frantic efforts were to no avail and the whirlpool swept a wave over the top of her head. Jody managed to battle her way to the surface again, only to be dragged under once more.

"Oh, no," she spluttered, knowing that she was seconds away from being drowned as she swallowed a mouthful of the swirling water.

The current was simply too fierce for her to overcome. "Help!" she cried out. "Please help me." But there was nobody there to save her.

WARNING!

You will be 'hooked' if you read on, so you should be aware that there are some really scary bits as the story unfolds.

...don't say you haven't been warned!

CHAPTER TWO

'THAT will teach her a lesson,' thought Mr. Toby as he wiped the rain off his nose and hobbled back into his warm sitting room.

He wedged his bulky frame into his armchair next to a roaring fire, and told his cat: "Young people are such a nuisance. But that's one little girl who won't be troubling me again. "Even if she survives the whirlpool she won't ever dare to come knocking at my door any more. On that basis, perhaps I should fish her out of the water. What do you think, Wham? "It's a dilemma. She may look like an angel, but she is a silly, rude girl who needed to learn a lesson."

His big black cat Wham, now sitting near his master in front of the fire, pricked up his ears at the sound of his name without giving any indication of providing an answer.

"I know," said Mr. Toby to the unreceptive Wham. "Let's have some fun. I'll toss my lucky coin to decide the silly girl's fate." He thrust his right hand into the breast pocket of his black robe and brought out a large gold, gleaming coin. "Heads I fish her out, tails I leave her in," he mused, flipping the coin in the air and letting it fall on to the open palm of his right hand.

He glanced at the coin without too much concern and noted it had come down 'tails'. "Oh, well," he said. "I did my best. Nobody can say Hugo Toby is not fair, can they, Wham? "Now it's up to the girl herself whether she sinks or swims." He returned the coin to his pocket and sat back in his armchair, with the intention of going off to sleep. Yet there was something bothering Hugo Toby. A thought was buried at the back of his mind and it was tantalising him.

Wham roused his large black bulk and moved close enough to Mr. Toby to rub himself against his master's leg. But Mr. Toby pushed the animal away and went over in his mind what the girl had said to him.

Finally it triggered off another thought process and brought back what he was seeking to remember.

"Of course, Wham" he confided to the cat. "That's it. She was looking for a boy, and my brother Augustine has some boys working for him. Perhaps the boy she was searching for is one of them."

He used his walking stick to poke the fire, which caused sparks to fly and the flames to leap higher.

"Maybe I should tell Augustine. If that girl could find her way

here then it is possible that others will follow her."

He looked down at the cat, which meowed in the hope of getting some food. "What do you think, Wham?" asked Mr. Toby. "Should I send a message to Augustine by a flying letter? I think I will. Better still, I might even arrange to visit him this week.

"Augustine was telling me on the telephone that he thinks he has found the secret to everlasting life and wants to share it with me. So the sooner I go to see him the better. "Just imagine, Wham, how wonderful it would be if Augustine and I could live forever. Think how much badness we would be able to do," chuckled Mr. Toby.

At 56 years of age, Mr Toby was cutting back on his evil activities – 'Good grief,' he thought, 'it's ages since I made any pixies disappear or turned any goblins into mice.'

He did not share his younger brother's burning desire to rule the world, but if he could live forever, never growing older, it might recharge his batteries and make world domination more appealing to him.

Wham pushed himself against his master's leg again and received a rough stroke on the head for his troubles. The cat meowed once more, much louder this time.

"What do you want, Wham?" Mr. Toby asked. "I suppose you think it's time for you to have more 'prawnies'. You are a greedy boy, aren't you? You've done nothing to deserve them, but you shall have them anyway." The cat purred appreciatively and licked his lips.

As Mr. Toby rose from his chair, he found that another drop of rain had settled on his nose after trickling down from his forehead. It dripped on to his goatee beard, which covered a cluster of chins.

The obese Mr. Toby wiped the rain water off with his handkerchief and then reflected: "I suppose I should have sent the girl to Augustine so that she could work for him, too. Perhaps sending her to drown in the whirlpool was not such a good idea, but it was such fun. And I've got to have some pleasures, haven't I?" He was convulsed with laughter and had to wipe a tear from his eye.

"I'm sure Augustine will understand and not think me selfish. Who knows, the girl may even survive, though I very much doubt it.

"I mustn't upset myself about it – as I said when my doctor warned me of the stress if I married a young wife: 'If she dies, she dies'!"

CHAPTER THREE

THE water swirling around Jody was too strong for her to battle against it much longer.

She was dragged under by the current of the whirlpool for the third time and swallowed two more mouthfuls of water before she resurfaced.

'I'm too young to die,' she thought as she struggled to breathe and her life was about to be snuffed out before it had hardly begun.

Even at this time of crisis her mind was filled with something her parents had always taught her: 'If only I had heeded their advice not to go speaking to strangers.'

Knocking on Mr. Toby's door had been a very bad idea! Jody prayed for a miracle, though she told herself this was the end as the water splashed over her and the whirlpool began to pull her down once more.

But, just before the water could engulf her again, she raised her arms and looked up into the clear blue sky in which, amazingly, she saw a man emerge on a flying horse!

The man had a long white beard and white hair, partly covered by a pointed blue hat with silver stars, which matched his robe.

The horse was a beautiful white stallion, similar to one Jody had seen when visiting the circus with her parents, but the big difference was this animal had large wings that were enabling it to glide through the sky at lightening speed.

As the horse swooped closer the man astride him, on a bright red saddle, clicked his fingers and Jody was instantly lifted out of the water. She sailed through the air and finished up sitting behind her saviour.

"Hello," said the man in a warm voice. "I am Wiffle, the Wizard of Kindness, and this is my flying horse Nesbeth. How did you come to fall into the whirlpool?"

Jody looked at Wiffle's half turned bearded face but had to gasp for air before she could answer him. "I'm pleased to meet you. I'm Jody Richards," was all she could say at first as she held on tightly to the wizard's waist.

She eventually managed to add: "How I ended up in the whirlpool is not easy to explain."

Then, as she recovered, Jody found that the relief of being saved from drowning was being replaced with a stomach-churning fear of falling off the horse, which was flying so high that they seemed to be almost within touching distance of the clouds.

Nesbeth's smooth coat was as white as newly fallen snow, but Jody had no time to admire it. She clung on to Wiffle and tightened her legs around the horse to prevent herself from slipping off. At the same time her teeth were chattering, partly through cold, as she was still dripping wet – and partly through terror.

"Don't worry," called out the wizard soothingly. "We're about to land now. Then we'll get you dry and warm."

Nesbeth began to descend and Jody, plucking up the courage to look down, saw what appeared to be a delightful village green – though the grass was actually pink! Around it were dotted houses and cottages and, further on, there was a small shopping centre. Within seconds they were landing on the pink grass. Wiffle and a rather shaky Jody alighted from the horse and walked over to a nearby wooden seat to sit down.

"First things first," said Wiffle. "Let's dry you off." He clicked his fingers to make the water drain out of Jody's light blue dress. "Instant, dry cleaning" he chuckled.

"Now, tell me the story of how you came to be in the whirlpool."

"But where am I?" asked Jody anxiously. "I've never been her before, though I have dreamed about this place."

"You are in Tamila. It's a magical island inhabited by pixies, goblins, fairies and wizards – many good ones like myself, but also a few bad ones. Oh, and there are some troublesome witches, too. The island has a magic ring around it so nobody from the outside world knows it is here.

"Now tell me how you got here – and how you came to be in the whirlpool."

"I don't really know for certain," Jody confessed, slowly beginning to relax. "My brother James disappeared three weeks ago from our home in Bromley in Kent – that's in England. He told me he wanted to go on an adventure holiday in some far off country and then a few days later he went missing. But he's only 11 and has never gone off on his own before.

"I would lie awake at night wondering where he could be and wishing I could find him. When I eventually fell off to sleep two nights ago I dreamed about this place. It was a really deep dream and so spooky, but I became scared and woke up.

"Last night I had the same dream and actually saw a wizard waving his wand. I seemed to be lifted from my bed and the next thing I knew I was here.

"Unfortunately, I got lost and knocked on the door of a nasty wizard with a large stomach, long nose and black beard who I had seen in my first dream. I told him I was looking for James and he suggested I go to the whirlpool. Then he clicked his fingers and I found myself in the pool. It was like a nightmare."

"That's exactly what it was," Wiffle told her, grinning through his marvellous white beard. "It's all part of your dream, you see. You wanted to find James so much that you dreamed yourself here.

"Unluckily for you the first person you met was a bad tempered wizard. From the way you describe him it must have been Hugo Toby. He can be very nasty, I'm afraid. Fortunately, as you were only in a dream, he could not harm you permanently.

"Although your experience in the whirlpool seemed very real and awful to you, you would not have drowned because it was all part of your dream. Very soon you'll wake up and you'll be back home again."

"But while I'm in Tamila I'd like to stay and look for James," Jody insisted. "My parents are worried sick about him. They reported his disappearance to the police and believe he has been kidnapped. But the police haven't a clue where he is. I may have the best chance of finding him because I've got this feeling that he's here – the least I can do is look for him."

Wiffle raised his large white bushy eyebrows in mock disapproval. "Well, in that case you had better wish that your dream turns into reality. But I must warn you that if you do so, it means you are putting yourself in possible danger because the black wizards like Mr. Toby could then harm you. If you found yourself in danger again it would be real – not a dream."

"I'm more worried about finding James and then getting us both home again," Jody told him as Nesbeth folded his wings and began to nibble the pink grass.

"Well, I have the power to grant you two wishes," Wiffle offered. "The first can be that your time here is extended and is no longer a dream. The second wish you can use for whatever you want – so when the time comes it could take you back home. But I must point out there are two conditions."

"What are they?" asked Jody anxiously.

"You must not misuse the wishes I am granting you and you must tell people the truth about your reason for being here." "That's easy," Jody assured him. "I need the wishes to find my brother and get us home safely so I certainly won't misuse them. And I don't tell lies."

"Excellent," said Wiffle, rising from the wooden seat. "It is so important to be truthful and honest at all times."

"That's exactly what my father says," she told him.

"It's an excellent motto," Wiffle confirmed. He then muttered an incantation that Jody couldn't understand and told her: "I have granted you two wishes. Now you had better come with me to my house and see if I can find out anything about your brother."

Wiffle and Jody walked towards two attractive houses, one blue and one white, on the outskirts of the village a few yards away, with Nesbeth eventually following by trotting slowly behind them.

Jody was thoughtful. Finally she said: "I can never thank you enough for saving me from the whirlpool, even if it was only a dream. It certainly seemed very real to me. And thank you for your kindness in granting me two wishes. But couldn't I just wish that my brother James and I are both back home?" Wiffle sighed. "That will only be possible if you find him and if he wants to go with you. The problem is we have no idea where your brother might be. I know nobody called James so you will have to search for him. Then, if you do find him, you can use your second wish to transport you both home. Meanwhile, I'll give you some food and a hot drink to warm you up."

Wiffle led the way along a quaint little path, taking them to the two imposing houses, and opened a wooden gate leading to the front garden of the second building. Jody, her dress crumpled and dishevelled, followed him towards the front door of his stately looking house. Everything was white, including a large porch and six fluffy cats seated on it.

But before they reached the regal front door a lady followed them up the path and called to Wiffle in an upper crust, snobbish voice that registered strong disapproval.

"Mr. Wiffle," said the tall, assertive yet elegant middle-aged woman. She had the grace and stature of a duchess, but the aggression of a prowling lioness about to bare her teeth. "Mr. Wiffle, I really must protest.

"You have allowed your cats to roam on my lawn where they have left behind something quite unmentionable. As if that isn't bad enough your horse appears to have eaten my mushrooms and your parrot has used language that I simply cannot tolerate.

"Imagine my annoyance when I went into the garden today to pick some mushrooms for a nice omelette, only to find there were none there."

"I'm very sorry, Mrs. Parker-Smythe," Wiffle said, sympathetically. "Perhaps we could discuss this some other time because, as you can see, I have a young visitor. Meanwhile, I will have strong words with my cats, my horse and my parrot."

"I don't expect you to be flippant about this matter, Mr. Wiffle," replied Mrs. Parker-Smythe, shaking her head in disgust. "And the fewer strong words you use the better. I suspect it is your strong words that your parrot keeps repeating. If any of these things happen again I will come and see you immediately, Mr. Wiffle. Do I make myself clear?"

"Crystal clear, Mrs. Parker-Smythe," he said, suppressing a grin. "I am truly sorry."

Wiffle's outspoken neighbour now turned her attentions to the untidy Jody, whose brown locks were still dripping wet. "And I hope you are not one of those annoying children who make a lot of noise or cause a mess," she snapped. "I note with displeasure that you have already dripped water all the way up the path. Fancy getting your hair wet through – you silly girl."

Jody's bottom lip trembled and she had to fight to hold back the tears that were threatening to flow from her sparkling blue eyes, which for the second time within an hour opened far wider than usual to register her astonishment. "It was an accident," she managed to mumble.

"Ladies don't have accidents," came the curt reply. "I'm not a lady," Jody protested.

Mrs. Parker-Smythe looked at her with disdain. "And you never will be unless you show more refinement. Let me pass on to you the same advice I gave to my husband, Bobbykins, this morning. Only open your month when it is absolutely necessary. It's better that people merely think of you as ignorant – rather than you remove any trace of doubt."

With that Mrs. Parker-Smythe turned on her heel and marched back to her own house next door, tutting and muttering about "lack of thought for other people."

"I'm sorry about that," Wiffle told Jody, getting out his key and letting them both into the house.

"You wouldn't believe Mrs. Parker-Smythe once bred dogs would you? She used to enter them in shows, but she can't seem to stand anyone else's animals. So we don't see eye to eye because I love all animals. I even make allowances for her beast of a husband Bobbykins."

They both burst out laughing.

"Beast of a husband," squawked the parrot from the front room. "Bobbykins is a beast." That made Wiffle and Jody laugh even more.

The wizard showed Jody into a large yet cosy lounge, containing several bookcases, a few oil paintings and a beautifully carved grandfather clock.

He signalled her to sit on one of two large brown armchairs as the parrot gave an encore. Wiffle lamented: "I wouldn't mind, but my parrot doesn't get his bad language from me. He picks it up from Mrs. Parker-Smythe's husband who is always cursing when his wife is not within hearing distance." Jody did her best to pay attention, but she had sunk deep into the soft fabric of the armchair, which engulfed her like a velvet glove. She had to struggle to sit up.

Wiffle, oblivious to the girl's discomfort, continued: "To make matters worse Bobbykins is currently doing some DIY work in his house with a drill that woke me up at 7.30 this morning."

"Why don't you put a spell on him?" asked a voice so softly

it seemed to be talking in a whisper.

Jody strained to see who had spoken, but at first saw nobody. Then, as she managed to turn partly round, she spotted something above her head - and a pretty fairy, just a few inches tall, flew past her.

"As one of the elders of the Confederation of Wizards I can hardly go around using my magic to punish people can I, Heatherbelle?" Wiffle said, answering the fairy's question with one of his own. "And, surely you, a good fairy, should not be encouraging me to do so. No, the drilling will stop in a day or so when Bobbykins has finished his work." Turning to Jody, he added: "Let me introduce you to my fairy, Heatherbelle."

"Hello," said the fairy coming to rest on the top of the other armchair opposite that in which Jody was sitting.

"Pleased to meet you," Jody replied.

"I have a little job for you, Heatherbelle," Wiffle told the tiny creature.

"And what might that be, oh master?" asked Heatherbelle sarcastically. "Re-point your hat? Press your cloak? Or polish your wand?"

"You can do all those things later – this is something more important," Wiffle replied, rebuking her. "I want you to fly around the village to talk to some of the other fairies and find out if they have seen Jody's 11-year-old brother.

"She has come to Tamila to look for him. Can you help her by visiting some of your friends?"

"I can do better than that," said Heatherbelle. "I am going out with five fairies tonight and we are bound to come across some others. I'll ask them all and let you know what I find out in the morning."

CHAPTER FOUR

BEFORE Heatherbelle went out she made Jody and Wiffle a truly fantastic meal.

The wizard then showed his young guest some of the rare collectors' items in his smartly furnished home – including an ancient wand, made from a peacock's feather, which belonged to Wiffle's great grandfather, and a magic watch that could take the person wearing it back in time.

The wizard also told an enthralled Jody more about Tamila. "It can be a wonderful place," he said. "But there are drawbacks and dangers. The good wizards and fairies are always helpful and, although the pixies are mischievous, they are not really harmful. But the goblins can be nasty creatures and the bad wizards and witches perform some evil deeds.

"Hugo Toby used to have two servants called Max and Freda, who stole some of his jewellery. This came to light when they tried to sell it. They haven't been seen since, but apparently Hugo now has two mice in a cage which look remarkably like miniature versions of Max and Freda." When Jody's yawns revealed she was ready for bed Wiffle loaned her one of his nightshirts and took her to a delightfully pretty guest room.

But she still missed her own bedroom at home, small though it was, and her favourite teddy bear, Biff.

Sensing her concern, Wiffle said kindly: "Is there something I can get you?"

"I don't suppose you have a teddy bear?

"How many would you like?" he asked, smiling. He clicked his fingers and suddenly a dozen teddy bears appeared on the bed. One caught Jody's eye because it was bright orange and had only one ear. She picked it up and gave it a little hug.

"Wiffle," Jody called to him as the wizard said goodnight. "I'm worried about my parents – they don't know where I am. Goodness knows what they'll think when they find I'm missing as well as James."

"They won't be aware that you've gone yet," he assured her. "Tamila is a magical place with a 48-hour time difference from the outside world. That means you have gone back two days in time from England and you won't be missed until the day after tomorrow."

"How marvellous," she said. "With any luck I could find James by then, and we could both be on our way back home."

Jody slid down the bed and fell asleep as soon as her head touched the silk pink pillows.

She was woken up on the dot of 7.30 the next morning by the sound of drilling.

"What did I tell you?" asked Wiffle over the noise coming from next door when Jody entered the kitchen to join him for breakfast. "Bobbykins is drilling again next door. Never mind, we needed to get up early. I've an important meeting to attend and you want to get off to look for James. Come in and have some toast and porridge."

Jody, smothered by the wizard's long nightshirt, pushed the kitchen door open further without seeing Heatherbelle on the other side. The fairy had to flap her tiny wings frantically to avoid being hit.

"Whoops, sorry," said Jody, moving quickly away from the door and almost tripping over the nightshirt that was several sizes too big for her. "I didn't see you standing – I mean flying – there."

The fairy nodded her head in acknowledgement, causing fairy dust to cascade over the breakfast table and into Wiffle's bowl of porridge.

"Watch out," protested Wiffle. "All that stuff is going into my porridge." "It will do you good," said Heatherbelle. "My fairy dust will put some extra sparkle into you."

That was the cue for Wiffle's parrot to join in the conversation. "Extra sparkle, extra sparkle," the parrot, squawked. Heatherbelle turned to look at Jody through blurry eyes that revealed she had stayed up far too late with her friends the previous night. "I'm afraid none of the other fairies have seen your brother," she said, apologetically. "I gave them all the description you provided, but nobody could recall seeing an 11-year-old boy like him."

Wiffle sighed. He told Jody: "That means your brother is not in this village – otherwise one of the fairies would know about it. So if he is in Tamila he will probably be across the water on the Island of Visions, which will make it more difficult for you to find him."

"Why is that?" Jody asked, stepping over one of Wiffle's cats and taking a seat at the breakfast table. "Is it far away?" "No, not very far," Wiffle replied, passing her some special juice mixed from local exotic fruits. "The problem is the Island of Visions has been given that name because visitors who go there see all sorts of visions – none of which are real. As a result it can take strangers ages to find any place they are seeking.

"Unfortunately, I cannot stay with you today because there is a Convention of Wizards I must attend. But I could drop you off on the Island on my way if you are prepared to look around there on your own. You could get the ferry back." "That would be wonderful," Jody assured him, taking a sip of the special exotic fruit juice. It was better than anything she had ever tasted before in her life. She savoured the smooth liquor, and her face creased into a smile as she gulped it down.

"You seem to like our Zippy juice," observed Heatherbelle. "It comes from the Island of Visions. They also make some delightful chocolates there."

"I'll have to try them," enthused Jody, sipping some more Zippy juice.

"Just make sure you don't go near any witches or goblins," warned Wiffle. "They don't like children and they can be very spiteful."

CHAPTER FIVE

JODY prepared to join Wiffle in mounting Nesbeth as Heatherbelle fluttered overhead, bidding them a fond farewell.

"Here, take this," said the fairy, dropping a very small silver object into Jody's hand.

"What is it?" asked a curious Jody.

"It's a special silver whistle which Wiffle asked me to give you," said the fairy. "I've got to stay here while he is away, but if you get into any trouble just blow that whistle. I'll come to you and use my magic fairy dust to help you."

"Thank you very much," Jody replied, blowing the fairy a kiss, which almost swept her several feet in the air. "OOPS, sorry!"

Heatherbelle giggled and flew back to plant a kiss on Jody's cheek. "Do be careful," she warned. "Not only can you be fooled by the visions, but you could be tricked by the pixies and the goblins. And, remember, not all wizards are as nice as Wiffle."

"I'll be careful," Jody promised, putting the whistle into her pocket.

It did not take Nesbeth long to fly Wiffle and Jody to the Island of Visions, where they landed on a hill just beyond the island's narrow sandy beach.

The wizard pointed out a small jetty a few yards away where a ferry was moored. He explained that the ferry left once an hour to go back to the mainland. Wiffle also gave Jody directions to the shopping area, a golden nugget to buy herself food and drink – and some more advice.

She was to make sure that any shops she went into were the same inside as what they appeared to be on the outside – and if they were not she should leave.

Then Wiffle and Nesbeth took to the air and were gone. Jody walked towards the centre of the island with the wise wizard's words ringing in her ears: "Don't take anything you see for granted – it may just be a vision. And don't stay out after dark or you'll get lost. One person you can trust is Milo, the Bag Man. He walks about carrying his belongings in carrier bags from which he produces some quite amazing things. Milo usually eats his lunch by the large water fountain on the far side of the island.

"But if you run into any trouble use the magic whistle to call Heatherbelle. She will hear it no matter how far away she is and she will fly to you immediately."

Jody, having put the tiny whistle in her dress pocket together with the golden nugget, waved Wiffle goodbye. She then started walking briskly, eventually coming to a dusty road in which there were a sprinkling of dwellings, partly concealed by bright yellow bushes and pink trees.

As she walked on Jody felt increasingly thirsty and when she saw a café sign on the corner of a side-road she wandered towards it. The café had a bright blue frontage, with a large window revealing a few tables and chairs plus a line of stools on either side. Pale blue tablecloths and matching napkins made it appear inviting.

It looked just as nice inside as it did on the outside. So Jody opened the front door, causing a bell to ring, and walked in.

The pixie behind the counter was dressed from head to toe in green, including a hat with a bobble at the top. As he greeted her, Jody took the golden nugget from her pocket. "Have you come in for our golden nugget special?" the pixie asked, seeing the girl produce her coin.

"What is that exactly?" said Jody doubtfully.

"It's a bottle of Zap juice and a bag of Zingers. It's great value for money and the cheapest thing we sell," he assured her. Jody didn't know what Zap juice and Zingers were, but the juice was surely like the Zippy juice she had enjoyed at breakfast and Zingers sounded good. Besides, they were the only things in the café that a golden nugget would buy. "Oh, yes please," she answered.

The pixie took her golden nugget and told her to wait. He disappeared and suddenly so did the café! Instead, Jody found herself standing outside a petrol station.

She looked in disbelief at the forecourt on which there was only a single petrol pump. On it was hanging a sign which read 'Garage closed until petrol delivery at 2 pm.' Where the café counter had been was now a pay kiosk, but there was no trace of the pixie or anyone else.

On the ground next to Jody was a bag labelled 'Zingers' and a bottle marked 'Zap juice'. She picked up the 'Zap juice' and read the label, which said 'Add it to your petrol to make your car zap up the miles.'

"Oh, no," she cried. "It's some sort of special fuel. I can't drink this."

But then her face lit up. 'At least I have the bag of Zingers,' she thought. 'Perhaps there will be some cookies inside it.' Jody opened up the bag, only to find it contained six sachets. She read the wording on the sachets: 'Zingers – the special acid drops that put a zing under your car bonnet and burn away any rust'.

"These are no good either," fumed the frustrated girl.

Jody left the bottle of Zap juice on the garage forecourt, but stuffed the sachets of Zingers into one of her dress pockets as she trudged away. Her stomach was empty and so was her purse.

She was soon in the middle of the village centre, which consisted of a maze of winding streets and narrow passageways. These contained a mass of quaint little shops ranging from shoe repairers to grocery stores.

The streets were cluttered with people, pixies and a few goblins of all shapes and ages. Most of the people were shoppers who only succeeded in getting in the way of the pixies as they scurried to reach their destinations.

Jody passed several brightly coloured shops, including a large ice cream and soft drinks parlour with a charming wood-carved front. She peered in the large window to see countless containers of delicious-looking ice cream of all flavours from butterscotch and toffee to peach and lemon. The sight made Jody's mouth water, but she knew she could not have any. Yet surely this would be a good place to ask for a drink of water.

Plucking up her courage, she pushed open the door on which was a picture of a giant ice cream and bottle of pop. Jody went up to the person behind the counter, another green-clad pixie, and said: "I'm sorry to trouble you – I wonder if I could just have a glass of water, please."

But the stern-faced pixie, who was less than four foot tall with pointed ears and eyebrows that also arched upwards, told her: "You are not old enough to be inside a tavern, young lady. You are much too young to be in a place like this."

Jody protested: "It's not a tavern – this is a pop and ice cream parlour."

Yet when she turned round she realised to her horror that the shop was another vision and she was, indeed, inside a smoky, poorly lit bar!

The pixie, who she had thought was selling ice cream and pop, was, in fact, perched on a stool behind a bar counter on which were four pumps to enable him to pull pints of beer for his customers.

Grimy shelves at the back of the bar were full of different shaped bottles of various spirits. The largest and most colourful had an orange label identifying it as a special brew of Tamila whisky.

Jody looked around her and saw that the large window was no longer there – instead there was a smaller version containing frosted glass that let in little light.

"You'd better go," the pixie told her. "This is exclusively for adults. There are a couple of goblins in the other bar – and they hate children. If they see you in here when they are trying to enjoy a quiet drink there will be trouble."

Jody tried to make a hurried exit, but had lost her bearings in the dimly-lit saloon and, what she assumed to be the way out, took her through two doors into a kitchen where two pixies were working.

One of them, who appeared to be in charge, looked up and asked her: "Have you come to help us with the washing-up?"

"No," she stammered. "I am looking for my brother and came in for a glass of water."

The pixie, who wore a bright red shirt and gaudy skin-tight leggings with red and yellow hoops, said: "I'll give you a glass of water and tell you whatever I know about your brother if you do some washing-up."

"Have you seen my brother?" Jody asked hopefully. "He's got blond, wavy hair and big blue eyes like mine. But he is a year older than me."

"I might have done," said the pixie. "I might well have done. So have we got a deal?"

"All right, I'll do some washing-up for you if you tell me what you know" Jody agreed.

Only after she had spoken did she look across to the long metal sink where she saw almost a hundred dirty beer glasses, mugs and plates. "Oh, no," she sighed. "What have I let myself in for?"

After receiving a glass of water she was given the task of washing all the glasses and mugs – and then the plates as well. By the time she had finished her fingers were red and sore.

"OK," Jody said to the pixie in the red shirt. "I've done the washing-up. Now can you please tell me where my brother is?"

"Tell me again what he looks like," said the mischievous little imp.

Jody repeated James's description.

"Haven't seen him," replied the pixie, bursting into roars of laughter. The other pixie who was working in the kitchen, cooking on a large, greasy oven, joined in the merriment. "You naughty, pixie," Jody cried. "You tricked me into doing all that work and you've told me nothing."

"I didn't trick you," he insisted. "I said I'd tell you what I know about your brother. Unfortunately, I don't know anything." Jody felt her face go bright red with embarrassment and anger. She just wanted to get out of the horrid tavern as soon as possible, and marched through the nearest door. But it led down a passageway and when she got to the end of it she found herself peering into a small private room, with thick wooden beams protruding from a low ceiling and plastered walls that were so old they were flaking badly.

The only occupants in the room were two strange looking goblins.

Wiffle's warning immediately came into Jody's head: "Goblins don't like children and they can be very spiteful." This pair certainly looked spiteful!

CHAPTER SIX

THE goblins, who sat huddled round a plain wooden table, both had large pointed ears, short legs and knobbly hands. One of them was an ugly, squint-eyed fellow with a mop of untidy hair poking out from a wide-brimmed hat. He was dressed in a short, grey tunic and black boots that only came just above his ankles.

The other goblin was plumper, with big rosy cheeks, and was completely bald. He also wore a grey tunic, but his black boots were much longer.

"So," the plump goblin named Bodger was saying, putting down the mug of beer from which he had been drinking. "You say our master is about to discover the secret of everlasting life."

"That's right," replied his ugly companion called Enoch. "I heard him talking to his brother on the telephone. He told him he had found the formula to make a secret potion that will keep them both alive forever. He has been collecting all the ingredients and has simply to mix them together in the correct portions. Do you realise, Bodger, how valuable that formula would be?"

Jody kept herself hidden in the shadow of the passageway as she listened to their conversation.

Bodger was now saying: "Yes, it would be worth a fortune. As soon as our master has mixed it we should steal some of it from him and sell it. What do you think, Enoch?"

"I agree," said his friend who then became the victim of a sneezing fit. He sneezed five times before he was able to carry on. "Blast that cold of mine. Never mind. The fact is, my dear Bodger, I am several steps ahead of you.

"I have already spoken to one of the witches who live on the far side of the island where they practice all sorts of evil sorcery. I have arranged for her to come and see me here this very afternoon to discuss whether she would be interested in buying the formula.

"I have told her that so far I have only been able to locate the main two ingredients, which are in the master's storeroom in the castle. He has yet to mix them with another potion, which he has hidden in a secret hiding place.

"But the witch thinks the other ingredient is most likely to be one from a certain range of potions, and she is bringing a few concoctions with her. I can then take them and try mixing each of them with the ingredients in the storeroom." "So," mused Bodger. "We might be able to discover the formula ourselves."

"That's right," Enoch confirmed, excitedly. "If we can it will save us searching for the master's secret hiding place. Instead, all we'll have to do is go into the storeroom and help ourselves from the barrels containing the main two ingredients.

"But we'll have to be very careful. We must not take too much – otherwise our master will know we have stolen it. And then he would put a terrible spell on us like he did with his last guard, Stinky. He turned Stinky into a skunk and drowned him!"

"What did Stinky do to warrant such a dreadful fate?" asked Bodger, his eyes wide open in fright.

"Nothing," said Enoch, supping his glass of ale. "He just stunk, that's all.

"The master told him to stop smelling and when he didn't the master said 'If you are going to smell like a skunk you can be a skunk'.

"Unfortunately, he then smelt even worse because he wet himself with fear, so the master drowned him in gallons of perfume. At least in death he smelt better than he had ever done in life."

Bodger gulped incredulously. "Perhaps it's not worth the risk of us stealing the ingredients," he spluttered, beads of sweat coming from his bald head.

"Don't be silly," Enoch told him with a scowl that caused his squinting eyes to almost close. "This formula could make us rich beyond belief. Providing we only take some of the ingredients the master will be none the wiser. Then we could sell the formula to the witches – they would reward us handsomely. And by using the formula we could also live for ever."

"In that case count me in," said Bodger. "But I can't stay here talking to you much longer. I'm supposed to be patrolling the castle grounds and the forest. If the master should find I'm not on duty there will be hell to pay."

"Don't worry," Enoch assured him, looking at his watch. "It's almost mid-day and the master will be about to eat his lunch. Let's go to the bar and order another drink."

"Just one," said Bodger. "But I must go to the toilet first." With that he got up and walked towards the passageway in which Jody was standing. At first she was gripped by fear and unable to move. The two goblins would be furious to find she had overheard their plans.

She wondered whether she should blow the silver whistle Heatherbelle had given her and summons the fairy to help her. Jody actually pulled it out of her pocket. But she did not know how long it would take the fairy to arrive, and if she blew the whistle it would only attract the attention of everyone in the bar.

So Jody quickly dismissed the idea and put the whistle back again. Instead, she forced herself to retreat down the passage and, to her relief, found a door on the right through which she quickly disappeared just as the goblin approached.

The frantic girl prayed that he had not seen her double back as she entered a gloomy room and quickly crossed to another door on the far side of it. She was delighted to find that it opened on to a yard behind the kitchen.

She couldn't bring herself to go into the kitchen again, but at the end of the yard was a wall that was not too high for her to climb.

At last she could escape from this wretched tavern.

CHAPTER SEVEN

JODY raced across the yard and climbed on a beer crate to get to the top of the wall without too much difficulty.

The wind blew Jody's gleaming golden-brown hair into her face, slightly blurring her vision and distracting her. But she ignored it.

She was so thankful to get away from the tavern and the horrid goblins that, without looking, she allowed herself to drop down the other side of the wall – right on top of an old woman!

"Ouch!," yelled the woman, toppling over and rolling on the ground, causing her grey coat to be covered in dirt from the side road along which she had been walking.

"I'm so sorry," said Jody, aghast. She got to her feet and quickly bent down to help up the dishevelled woman, whose stern-looking, wrinkled face suggested she was not just old

– she was ancient!

The hag, whose stand-out features were an extended chin and misshapen nose, had wrinkles on top of wrinkles – except where there were warts.

But what was more disturbing for Jody was that, in leaning over, she caused the magic whistle to fall out of her dress pocket – and watched in dismay as it dropped straight into a drain by the roadside.

"Oh, no!" she cried. "I've lost my whistle."

"You wicked girl," the woman shrieked. "You've just knocked me over and all you can think of is your whistle." She stood up slowly and rose to her full height – all five foot two inches of it.

Jody, finding herself staring at the woman's wrinkles and warts, became embarrassed and racked with guilt. Her beauty spot swelled as her cheeks went bright red.

"I didn't mean to be unfeeling," she explained. "It was just that the whistle was given to me to summons help if I needed it while searching for my brother James."

"How careless of you to lose him," chided the old dear, chuckling.

"No, you don't understand," said Jody.

This met with more displeasure from the woman, who knocked Jody's hand away when the girl tried to brush the dirt off her coat.

"Does looking for your brother entitle you to jump off walls? she demanded.

"There was a good reason why I did that, but it's a long story," Jody began. "Perhaps I should give you a full explanation. "My name is Jody Richards and I'm from a country called England. My brother James disappeared from our home and I came here to look for him. He's been gone three weeks now."

"I'm not interested in your brother or your whistle," the woman snapped.

She then checked her coat pocket and withdrew from it three glass tubes. They had clearly been broken by Jody falling on top of her and the liquid they contained had dripped all over the inside of the old dear's coat.

"A million curses," uttered the hag. "You have caused these tubes to break and all the potions I spent hours mixing have drained away."

She glared at the frightened young girl in front of her, fixing Jody with the meanest of stares from her steely grey eyes. Jody was terrified. "You..." she stuttered. "You're a witch aren't you?"

"That's right, dear" said the woman, gleefully. "There's no fooling you is there? I might as well dispense with my disguise."

With that she clapped her bony hands together and a blue mist engulfed her, followed by a red glow. It cleared in an instant to reveal that the old lady's grey coat had been replaced by a black cape, and a pointed hat had suddenly appeared on her head.

Jody stared in disbelief.

Adjusting her hat, the woman demanded: "Just because I'm a witch does that excuse you from jumping on top of me?"

"No," said Jody, full of guilt.

"And does it give you the right to break the glass tubes in which I was carrying special potions?"

"No," answered Jody, sorrowfully. "I'm sorry. Were they very valuable?"

"I'll never know now how valuable they might have been," the witch snapped. "I was about to deliver them to a goblin so that he could mix them with special ingredients he has to see if the two together produced the right formula. Now I'll have to start again.

"You need to be taught a lesson young lady. I'm going to place a curse on you."

"Please don't," pleaded Jody.

But her protest was to no avail. The witch drew out a black wand from her cape and waved it menacingly.

"Just so that you don't think I'm being mean I'll even give you a choice of curses," the old woman said, smiling, which caused the sagging skin around her mouth to fold into a dozen creases. "Let nobody say that Huffy Haggard is unfair."

"Huffy Haggard? Is that your name?" asked Jody.

"Yes, it is," growled the witch, the smile disappearing from her wrinkled face, the condition of which proved she was aptly named. "Are you suggesting that there is something wrong with it?"

"No, not at all," Jody said, not seeking to offend the witch any further. "It's just that it's a little unusual."

"Well," Huffy Haggard replied. "If you want to know what 'unusual' really is I'll show you.

'Oh, dear,' thought Jody. 'I've spoken out of turn again.' What was it Mrs. Parker-Smythe had said?

"Only open your month when it is absolutely necessary. It's better that people merely think of you as ignorant – rather than you remove any trace of doubt."

The witch was now uttering some magic chant that sounded like "Inca, Inca, Inca – Alzibar, Alzibar, Alzibar" and waving her wand in a large circle

Then she added words that caused Jody's blood to go cold. "I call upon the spirits to make this girl's big toes turn into snails."

Jody looked down at her opened-toed sandals and recoiled in terror at the sight of her big toes, which were now no longer toes – but large, slimy snails.

"No, no," she yelled, a feeling of utter revulsion sweeping over her.

"No?" the old lady questioned, chuckling. "Very well, then, let's try something else."

Huffy waved her wand and said: "Instead of snails on her toes, let me turn the end of every hair on her head into a worm."

Jody was petrified. She could see her big toes had been restored to normal, but she dared not put her hands up to her head to confirm worms were now there. Jody quickly found she didn't need to do so because she could feel the creatures wriggling as if she had been given live hair extensions.

"Take them away! Please take them away!" she shouted hysterically.

"I presume you don't like that spell, either," said the witch as Jody continued to scream. "My, you are a fuss pot, aren't you? All right, all right, keep your hair on! I'll cancel that spell, too. But you've run out of choices so you'll be stuck with the next one."

"Please just get them off my head," screamed Jody, frantically trying to remove the worms herself with her hands. "PLEASE! This is so awful I just can't stand it" Huffy swished the wand again and said: "Restore her hair to normal." Instantly, the worms were gone.

Jody ran her hands through her hair to make quite sure the worms were no longer there. A feeling of relief swept over her.

"Now," the witch mused. "What shall I make the final spell?" "Please don't let it be anything crawly or slimy," Jody begged, the worms on her hair having made her feel quite sick. "Very well," Huffy replied, obviously enjoying herself. "We'll simply settle for a nose job just like Pinocchio's. I call upon the spirits to make this girl's nose grow half and inch. And to cause it to grow a further half inch every time she does not carry out my instructions."

Jody felt her nose and, to her horror, found it had become half an inch longer.

The witch told her: "From now on every time you meet someone you will tell them: 'I am a very naughty girl who cannot be trusted.'

"If you fail to do so your nose will grow another half inch. And if you ever jump off another wall your nose will become twice as big."

"Oh, no," cried Jody, unable to stop herself from crying. But Huffy took no notice. Instead, she scurried away towards the main entrance to the tavern, calling over her shoulder: "Let that be a lesson to you."

CHAPTER EIGHT

JODY walked around in a trance, repeatedly feeling her extended nose and crying uncontrollably. Eventually, she came across a large blue fountain and peered into the clear water it was sprinkling on to a stone bowl so that she could study her reflection.

Even an extra half an inch made an enormous difference and her nose felt massive every time she touched it.

As she inspected it for the umpteenth time she couldn't prevent herself bursting out crying again. She didn't notice that she was being watched by a large, jovial man, sitting on a stone wall next to the fountain, eating a pie. He had long whiskers growing from under his nostrils like a giant moustache, but no beard. Beside him were three carrier bags. "Are you all right?" he asked.

Jody was startled and alarmed. She knew she must say what the witch had told her or else her nose would grow even longer. But could she remember the exact words? She concentrated hard.

"I asked if you were all right?" the man repeated, firmly but not unkindly.

Jody began to panic. She must speak, but if she got the words wrong her nose would grow another half inch. Finally she spluttered: "I am a very naughty girl who cannot be trusted." Jody felt her nose and was so relieved to find that it had not grown – but she was also embarrassed at what she had said.

"Are you, indeed! That means you are like most children I have come across," her new companion replied, laughing. Then Jody recalled what Wiffle had told her about a man with carrier bags who ate his lunch by a water fountain. "Excuse me," she inquired of the eccentric stranger. "Are you the Bag Man?"

He looked up at her rather annoyed. "How rude of you. You interrupt my lunch with your crying and then call me the Bag Man," he muttered. "You young people have no manners." 'Oh, no,' thought Jody. 'I've upset him.'

Mr. Toby's words came back to haunt her: "You are an extremely rude little girl."

If only she gave more thought to what she was going to say. She was tempted to run away, but became rooted to the spot. And when Jody opened her mouth to say sorry she found it hard to get the words out. Finally, she stuttered: "I'm sorry sir. I didn't mean to be rude. Wiffle did tell me your name, but I'm afraid I've forgotten it."

"Ah," sighed the man. "I suppose Wiffle told you I was known as the Bag Man. People usually only call me that behind my back. My real name is Milo. What do you want with me?" Jody explained to the Bag Man how she was looking for her brother, but had fallen foul of some nasty pixies and an evil witch who had made her nose grow a half inch longer. To make matters worse nobody had seen James and she had given away her golden nugget without getting any food – and then lost her magic whistle.

"So, you're hungry are you?" the Bag Man asked, suppressing a smile.

"Yes, sir," replied Jody.

"Then, I'd better find something for you to eat," he replied. The Bag Man went over to his three carrier bags and searched through the contents in one of them. Then, after two abortive attempts, he pulled out an uncooked chicken. "No, that's no good," he muttered, putting it back and finding a dozen raw sausages strung together. "That won't do, either," he said, placing them back in the bag. Finally, he triumphantly produced a crumpled beef sandwich, which he offered to an amazed Jody.

Despite the hunger pangs she was experiencing, Jody's first inclination was to refuse it, but she did not want to offend the Bag Man again. So she accepted the battered sandwich and, after thanking him profusely, she was obliged to eat it. To her surprise it tasted rather nice.

He delved in his bag again to produce a large bottle of lemonade and a glass, which he gave her to drink from. "Unfortunately, there is nothing I can do about your nose, though it does not look too bad," the Bag Man comforted. "What I may be able to do is tell you if I've seen your brother. Why don't you draw me a picture of what he looks like? Hold on, I've got some paper and a pencil somewhere." He then ferreted in another carrier bag until he eventually came across a pad of pink paper and a pencil, which he offered to her.

Jody managed to draw a rough sketch of James as he looked when she last saw him and gave it to the Bag Man. No sooner had he glanced at it than the Bag Man shouted "Uga Oooo!"

"What does that mean?" inquired a startled Jody.

"It's just my way of expressing my amazement," the Bag Man explained. "I've actually seen a boy similar to this, although he looks a little older than your drawing. He was in the forest and I believe he was working for Augustine Toby." Jody's cry of joy was suddenly stifled as the name Toby was mentioned. "You mean the fat, nasty wizard with a black beard and a long nose like mine?" she asked.

"No," the Bag Man answered. "That is Hugo Toby. This is his brother Augustine Toby, known as Augustine The Awful because he is even worse than Hugo. He's not just bad tempered like Hugo, he is also very cruel and extremely vicious."

"Oh, poor James," she cried. "How terrible for him to be working for such a horrid wizard."

"If the boy I saw is your brother, you will find it very hard to talk to him because those who work for Augustine The Awful in the forest are guarded by huge, ferocious dogs." "But I must find him," insisted Jody. "I can use a wish that Wiffle has granted me to take James home. Can you tell me how to get to Augustine The Awful's home? Perhaps if I ask him nicely he will let me see James."

The Bag Man shook his head. "I'm afraid you are very naive to think that," he replied. "Augustine The Awful has probably tricked your brother and other children into working for him against their will so he's hardly likely to let you talk to James. It wouldn't be wise to go to Augustine The Awful's castle, as you would be in great danger. If I were you I would keep as far away from Augustine The Awful as possible. I know to my cost how wicked he can be."

"What do you mean?" Jody inquired.

"Not long after I became a fully fledged wizard I got involved in a heated row with Augustine The Awful. We had a battle of wills in which he used his greater experience and knowledge to beat me. He took away most of my magical powers and destroyed my home.

"The only possessions I now have are those in these bags.

But he has done even worse things to others.

"He has turned pixies into frogs, reduced his rivals to the size of insects and surrounded his castle with a magical stream that causes whoever walks into it to have their memories wiped out.

"He even turned one goblin into a skunk and drowned him in perfume – just because he was smelly."

"Then Augustine The Awful must be the 'master' who those two goblins in the tavern were talking about," Jody said. "One of them mentioned how he had turned a guard into a skunk."

"What were you doing in a tavern?" the Bag Man scolded. "You're too young to go into places like that."

"Don't you start," Jody rebuked him in what was meant as a joke.

"Now, you're being rude again," said The Bag Man. "That will have to go into the book."

"What book?" she asked.

"The journal I keep in my mind in which I write all the good things in red and all the bad things in black. That is definitely a black mark against you."

"I'm sorry, I didn't mean to upset you Bag Man...I mean Milo," she apologised. "I only went into the tavern because I thought it was an ice cream and lemonade parlour. Then I was tricked into washing up loads and loads of dirty beer glasses.

"When I finally finished I came across a private room in which two goblins were talking about their master discovering a formula for everlasting life. They were planning to steal the ingredients."

"Were they now?" mused the Bag Man. "So Augustine The Awful wants to live for ever. I can't think of anything more revolting... it's enough to..."

"I really must try to find James," Jody interrupted. "I think I should go to the forest now and see if he is working there. Can you tell me the way?"

"Very well," he replied. "In fact, I'll do better than that – I'll take you there."

"Oh, if you could help me, I'd be so grateful," Jody told him. "We must be very careful that Augustine The Awful's guard doesn't spot us," warned the Bag Man.

"We don't have to worry about him," replied Jody. "He's still drinking in the tavern with his colleague."

"But we do have to worry about the guard dogs," the Bag Man reminded her. "We have to think of a way to stop them attacking us."

CHAPTER NINE

HUFFY HAGGARD was pleased to note that the tavern bars were dark and not over-crowded. There were now three other goblins in the private bar, but she made her way over to the corner table at which Enoch was seated with Bodger and introduced herself.

"What made you so sure it was us?" asked Enoch.

"I had no trouble spotting you two characters," she said, fixing both of them with a piercing stare. "You are the shiftiest looking customers in the place."

"There's no need to be rude," said Enoch. "We are in a position to do you a big favour."

"So you tell me," said the witch, sitting on a chair opposite them. "Would you gentlemen like another drink?"

"Yes please," said Bodger. "I'll go to the bar and order them if you like."

"No need," replied Huffy, firmly. She clapped her hands and immediately the two nearly empty beer glasses on the table were refilled. She repeated the movement together with a few mumbled words and a glass of witches' brew appeared for herself. "So much better than paying," she said, chuckling. "And I find it so embarrassing asking for witches' brew.

"In fact, I rarely dress as a witch when I come into places like this – people are so prejudiced towards us witches. But an unfortunate incident outside caused me to reveal myself. "Now what more can you tell me about this formula Augustine The Awful has discovered that can give everlasting life?" Enoch leaned forward so that he was nearer to the witch and could keep his voice low. But at that moment he was overcome by one of his sneezing fits and, despite hurriedly putting his hand over his swollen nose, he very nearly blew the witch's hat off her head.

"Sorry," he apologised. "I'm very sorry."

"You will be," the old hag warned. "I could arrange for you to have a big red nose and big ears to go with it. Oh, silly me, you've already got them, haven't you?

"Just make sure you cut out that sneezing. I know all about you goblins – how your smile can curdle the blood and your laugh can sour the milk and cause fruit to fall from the trees. So I'm on my guard."

Undaunted, Enoch continued: "As I explained to you before, I know where the main two ingredients are for the formula for everlasting life. But my master Augustine The Awful has the other ingredient hidden in a secret place. It's just a question of following him to find out where that place is." "Where are the main two ingredients kept?" the old woman asked, eager for knowledge.

"In barrels in the storeroom of the castle," Bodger revealed, without putting his brain into gear. He was about to say more, but he shut up quickly when he saw that Enoch was glaring at him. "You said you thought you might know what some of the ingredients are," Enoch muttered to the witch. "If you have brought them I can mix them with those in the castle storeroom and see if they work. That is providing you agree to pay me and Bodger one thousand golden nuggets." "The money is no problem," the witch replied, dismissively. "I did bring three different potions with me so that you could try mixing each of them with those in the castle, but some silly girl jumped on top of me and broke the glass tubes I was carrying them in. It means I will have to make some more.

"That stupid girl! All she could think about was losing her whistle and finding her long lost brother."

"Her brother?" asked Enoch. "Did she say how old he was or what he was called?"

"I wasn't really listening," answered Huffy. "I think she said his name was James and her name was Jody. Why do you ask?"

"Augustine The Awful has three boys working for him in the forest and one of them is called James," answered Bodger, before Enoch could speak. "I'm supposed to be guarding them. I must get back to the forest at once."

"I'll come with you," said Enoch. "And I'll also call Augustine The Awful on the voice box he gave me to alert him about the girl."

Turning to the witch, he added: "We'd better meet again when you've mixed some more potions or if, in the meantime, I can discover the rest of the formula."

Huffy nodded and promised: "If you find all the ingredients for the secret potion I'll increase your fee."

"By how much?" asked Enoch.

"Let's say two thousand golden nuggets – and a very big bonus if it takes all my wrinkles away.."

CHAPTER TEN

THE Bag Man gathered up his carrier bags and led Jody over a bridge towards the forest. On the way he explained to her how dreadful it was to lose his powers in a battle of wills against Augustine The Awful.

"Can't you get them back?" she asked.

"Only if I can discover a way to lift the spell Augustine The Awful placed on me – and that's most unlikely," the Bag Man explained.

"Fortunately, I've got a lot of useful things stored in my bags. And I still have a couple of basic powers left. If I click my fingers I can produce food and drink, and I can also..." He was interrupted by a loud crack of thunder and a fierce flash of lightning.

"Uga, Oooo," yelled the Bag Man. "We'd better hurry to get under the shelter of the trees in the forest before it starts to rain."

They quickly reached the forest, which was a mass of pink – rather than green – leaves.

No sooner had they got there than they were greeted by another clap of thunder and large drops of red rain fell down on them.

"It always seems to be raining here," Jody moaned as they sheltered under a gigantic tree with wide leaves hanging from its many branches.

"That's because this is the rain season," the Bag Man explained. "But it is probably only a shower – it won't last long."

When the rain had subsided they made their way through a cluster of pink leaves from overhanging branches until they were surrounded by trees.

"This way", the Bag Man urged as another clap of thunder sounded above them.

Eventually, they could hear some activity ahead. But, as they got nearer, there was also the sound of dogs barking. The dogs – bigger and more ferocious than any Pit Bull Terriers – were now coming into view.

"What can we do to prevent them attacking us?" asked Jody.

"I can handle that," replied the Bag Man. He clicked his fingers and suddenly six pieces of steak appeared on the ground in front of them.

"As I was telling you, I can still do basic magic like producing food," he said.

The Bag Man then delved into one of his bags and rummaged around until he found a large tube. He unscrewed the top from it and squeezed out a green substance, which he smeared on the steak. Then, walking towards the yelping dogs, he threw each of them a large juicy piece of meat. The hungry animals immediately started to devour it.

"But as soon as they've eaten the meat they'll attack us," protested Jody.

"I don't think so," chided the Bag Man. "I've added a large dose of sleeping potion and they should soon be flat out." No sooner had he spoken than the dogs began to yawn and fall asleep.

After walking a few steps further Jody and the Bag Man came to a small clearing and in front of them was a cluster of giant red trees – much taller than those they had passed already. They were at least 500 feet in height and at the top were a mass of leaves and branches containing golden berries.

Jody gasped in amazement – she had never seen trees so tall and imposing.

When they got nearer they could see three boys – two in the process of climbing up the trees and one climbing down. All had ropes and harnesses to help them.

The boy who was coming down had a large bag over his shoulder, which was full of sprigs containing golden berries. The bag also had an axe and a pair of clippers poking out of it. The lad finally dropped to the ground, freed himself from the rope that had held him and began emptying the berries into a large wooden cart. As they approached him, Jody could see that he had blond hair and closely resembled her brother. "James," she yelled. "Is that you?"

Then she began to panic as she remembered the witch's curse and what she had been told to say to everyone she met. Jody hurriedly added: "I am a very naughty girl who cannot be trusted." She felt her nose to make sure it had not grown. Fortunately, it hadn't.

"Don't tell him that," snapped the Bag Man.

"I can't help it," Jody insisted. "It's part of the witch's curse on me."

The boy turned round sharply, and allowed his bag to fall by his side. He looked at Jody and the wizard perplexed. "James, it IS you," she called out again and ran up to him. But as Jody hugged him in a warm embrace the boy pulled back, startled.

"What's the matter?" she cried as he stared at her blankly and the other two boys looked down from their trees, anxiously. "Why are you grabbing me?" he asked.

"James, don't you recognise me? It's me – your sister Jody," she told him. "Perhaps it's because my nose has got bigger. I knocked over a witch who put a spell on me by making my nose grow an extra half an inch. She has forced me to tell anybody I meet that they cannot trust me – but you can." The boy looked bewildered and insisted: "I don't know you. It's nothing to do with the size of your nose. I don't have a sister."

"How can you say that?" Jody demanded, and burst out crying.

The Bag Man comforted her and explained: "I told you Augustine The Awful can erase people's memories – that's obviously what he has done to your brother."

"Of course," acknowledged Jody, wiping her eyes. Then, turning to James, she urged: "Even if you don't remember me you must believe what I'm telling you. I'm your sister and I've come to take you back home to our parents. So please come with me now."

"No," stressed James, his bright blue eyes showing grave concern. "Augustine Toby will be very angry if I leave and he's extremely nasty when he's angry. That's why people call him Augustine The Awful. He always has dogs patrolling this area, with a goblin who will report us if he sees we are not keeping busy. Now please excuse me – I've got work to do."

"But surely you don't like climbing trees all day long," argued Jody. "You would be so much happier if you came home with me."

"I'm not just climbing trees," James corrected her. "We're cutting down branches of golden berries at the top of the trees and then taking them to Augustine Toby. We've also had to go swimming and diving to collect plant life from the bottom of the river for him.

"But you are right – I hate doing this work every day. At first it's great to climb trees but doing it hour after hour every day is rather boring and very tiring. The berries are hard to dislodge so we have to cut them off with an axe.

"Even so, why should I come with you when I don't even know you and have no idea where we would be going?" Just then there was another flash of lightning and one of the six dogs began to stir. "We'd better go," said the Bag Man, picking up the three carrier bags he had rested on the ground. "The dogs will be awake soon."

Jody tried to reason with James. "Look, you've got to trust me. Please come with me," she pleaded. "A very kind wizard called Wiffle has granted me a wish which I can use to get us home – will you come?"

"You keep talking about me coming home with you – I don't even know where you live," James objected. "If I knew I might come with you."

Suddenly there was a noise of rustling leaves and a broken twig behind them. Two startled birds – similar to pigeons only much larger – took off in fright and a squirrel scampered up a tree to escape the approaching footsteps. Jody, James and the Bag Man turned to see the formidable, grotesque figure of Augustine The Awful emerge and tower over them.

He was thinner, taller, nastier and even more intimidating than his brother Hugo. Unlike Hugo's choice of a loose- fitting robe, Augustine wore a black tailored costume. Next to him were the two goblins Jody had seen in the tavern.

But Jody couldn't stop staring at Augustine The Awful. She had never seen anyone look so cruel and callous.

He had three black tufts of hair on an otherwise bald head and thick rubbery lips that were twisted in a scowl.

Just the sight of his sinister features and evil black eyes – two large, deep pools of emptiness – caused Jody's muscles to tighten and stomach to churn.

If any further warning was needed it came when the tiny beauty spot on her left cheek began to itch as it always did when she was in danger.

What struck her most was the sheer size of this dreadful looking wizard. She had once seen a man on television who had been labelled a giant because he was 6ft 6in tall, but Augustine The Awful seemed much taller than that!

"Uga Oooo," shrieked a clearly shaken Bag Man, jumping almost out of his shoes.

CHAPTER ELEVEN

"ZENDA, I'm back," shouted Huffy Haggard, entering the inner sanctum of her cavern, built inside a mass of rock.

Her stark 'living room' – containing only basic wooden furniture – was lit up by lanterns hanging from the rugged walls and the glowing embers of a dwindling fire that had been made hours earlier in what passed for a hearth.

There was no reply, but the witch could tell her daughter was in because of the sound of disco music coming from the tunnel to her right. "Zenda," she bellowed. "Turn that noise off at once and come here – or I'll put a spell on you." In a luxuriously decorated room further down the passage a drop-dead gorgeous female, looking no older than 25, reluctantly eased herself out of her leather arm chair and sauntered across her white fur carpet in black diamond- studded high heeled shoes to reach her multi-decked music centre. One of her long, slender fingers, coated with black nail varnish, pressed the 'stop' button.

The blast of the heavy disco beat suddenly cut out, and seconds later Zenda entered through a door of solid rock after pressing a lever on her side of the wall to open it.

Although Zenda had natural beauty, her wild eyes, sharp bone structure and jet black hair gave more than a hint of her fiery character.

"Do give it a rest, mother," she said defiantly. "Now I'm a senior witch I'm no longer scared by your threats to put a spell on me. You'd better be careful I don't put one on you." "You should show your old, cantankerous mother more respect,

Zenda" Huffy told the younger witch, whose looks projected beauty and menace in equal quantities.

"You're certainly living up to your name, mother." "Huffy?" "No, Haggard!"

"That's a very unkind thing to say to your old mother." "I'm sorry. I'm just home sick," Zenda told her. "But you are living at home," Huffy exclaimed.

"Yes, and I'm sick of it," Zenda fired back. "You really should come into the 21st century, mother. It's quite ridiculous. I've got all the creature comforts in my room, including a hi-fi music centre, digital television, washing machine and microwave cooker, yet you're still living in this dump, sitting round a few burning lumps of wood and without even a proper carpet." She looked down in disdain at the rocky floor, covered only by a couple of plain rugs that were beginning to fray.

Huffy glared at her daughter, whose short leather skirt and top contrasted sharply with her own clothes, but she refused to rise to the bait. "That's your choice, Zenda, and this is mine," she said. "I've lived in this cavern for nearly 200 years and I'm set in my ways. You should respect that. Anyway I've got my clocks." She pointed to the far wall on which there was every type of clock imaginable – including cuckoo, chiming, weather, talking and grandfather.

"I have a really nice collection of time pieces."

"That's just a fetish, not a design statement," Zenda scoffed. "Enough of this nonsense," Huffy snapped. "I've got some news for you."

"What is it mother? Have you come across a new line in broomsticks?"

"Don't be so sarcastic or you'll be sorry," Huffy warned. "What I've come across is the secret potion for everlasting life."

"What?" said Zenda, taken aback. "You really know how to make us live for ever?"

"Not exactly," Huffy admitted, putting another two logs on the fire. "But I know a man who does. That nasty wizard in the big castle next to the forest, Augustine The Awful, has discovered the formula. And I have been talking to two of his goblins who can get it for us.

"The main two ingredients are kept in the castle's storeroom and when Augustine The Awful mixes them with the other potion that he has kept hidden then the formula will be complete. The goblins have agreed to steal it for us as soon as they can discover his hiding place.

"When we drink the potion we will never age again." "That's great!" exclaimed Zenda, showing more enthusiasm than her mother had seen for weeks. "Wait until I tell Auntie Leppe. Like you, she has been trying to discover the secret for years."

"I know," said Huffy. "Your Aunt and I have both experimented and we thought we had come very close to finding the formula. So maybe if we had the main ingredients from the castle storeroom we could come up with the other potion ourselves. In fact, I have been producing various potions of my own and one of them might be the answer."

"So why don't we just break into the castle storeroom and take the ingredients?"

"That would alert Augustine The Awful and then he would take extra precautions to ensure we never get our hands on the complete formula."

"Not if we send in our new assistant, Elsa," Zenda said, smiling slyly. "We could make her invisible and then she could get into the castle completely undetected."

"But she has only just finished learning the craft," Huffy pointed out. "She is not a fully fledged witch yet."

"She's finished her six-months training course and worked well under our supervision – she's got to be given her first solo mission sometime," insisted Zenda. "This should be a straight-forward task. Let me call her."

"OK, as long as she is very careful," Huffy agreed. "I don't know whether we can trust those two goblins to do the job properly. So we've nothing to lose by getting Elsa to take a look."

"Elsa," screeched Zenda, clapping her hands together. "Come hither. Your mistress is calling you."

There was a cloud of purple smoke and from it emerged an enormous witch with grotesque features, the worst of which were her bulging eyes. She was well over 6ft tall and looked huge despite her hunched shoulders, which caused her to stoop. "You called mistress," she said, bowing her head and lowering her unnerving eyes.

"Yes, Elsa," said Zenda. "We want you to try out the magic powers we have given you by flying to Augustine The Awful's castle. Go into his storeroom and bring back some special ingredients that are kept inside it."

"The ingredients are in barrels," Huffy said, pulling her cloak around her as a gust of cold wind blew through a gap in the roof, causing some flakes of rock to fall in front of her.

Ignoring Zenda's look of disgust, Huffy stressed: "Bring a drop of the ingredients from each barrel. But don't take too much – nobody must know you have been there."

"You can make yourself invisible to help you get into the castle," said Zenda.

"Yes," Elsa confirmed. "That will be no problem. Being invisible, I could even ring the castle's door bell and walk straight in when they open it to find nobody there!"

"No. I've got a better idea," Huffy told her. "Use your black magic to reduce yourself in size, Elsa, until you are as small as a bee. That will enable you to fly straight into the castle storeroom through the window. Once you are inside the storeroom you can revert to your normal size. You can then magic up two small bottles, put the special ingredients in them and transport yourself back here."

"Yes, that's an excellent plan, mother," Zenda agreed. "Your old mother isn't senile yet my dear," Huffy chided. "But I have almost completed a witch's normal life span and unless I find the secret of eternal life soon then I will die. So will Aunt Leppe and some of our friends. We must get our hands on that formula.

"I might have already come up with the missing potion, but a silly girl jumped off a wall on top of me today and broke the glass tubes in which I was carrying some samples.

"I told her she had caused my special potions to be destroyed, but she was more concerned about losing her whistle." "Who was this girl, mother?" Zenda asked, her grey eyes opening wider to express her concern.

"I don't know, dear," Huffy confessed. "She had long brown hair and told me her name was Jody. She was looking for her brother. The two goblins I met from the castle think her brother is one of the boys working for Augustine The Awful, but..."

She was interrupted by six of her clocks chiming. "That girl could be trouble," Zenda muttered.

Two more clocks suddenly chimed. Then the cuckoo clock joined in. Zenda glared at her mother. "Why was she jumping off a wall?" she asked.

"I've no idea," Huffy scoffed. "She was coming from the back of the tavern in which I met the goblins. She recognised me as a witch so I taught her a lesson for knocking me over and destroying the potions.

"I made her nose grow half an inch and it will continue to grow by the same measure unless she tells everyone she meets that she is a very naughty girl who cannot be trusted. I don't think anyone will take seriously anything she tells them."

Zenda looked alarmed. "Even so, this Jody might know too much and could be a threat to our plans," she insisted.

Elsa looked up, eager to help. "Perhaps you would like me to take care of her, mistress?" she asked.

"That would be a good idea," Huffy told her. "She is about ten years old, doe-eyed and quite pretty despite her longer nose, and has brown hair which is..."

Zenda interrupted her. "But your main task, Elsa, is to go into the castle and get us the ingredients for everlasting life from the storeroom."

"What shall I do if I see the girl on the way?" asked Elsa, keen to serve her mistress well now that she had been entrusted with her first solo mission.

"Put a spell on her," said Huffy. "Use your powers to send her straight here."

CHAPTER TWELVE

"WHAT are you doing here Milo and who is this girl?" Augustine The Awful demanded, glaring at the Bag Man and Jody in anger. His black eyes, which were blazing with even more menace than his brother's, narrowed and his pointed chin jutted out to register his displeasure.

Turning to glare at Jody, he told her: "I am Augustine Toby and I am the most powerful wizard in the whole of Tamila. Now tell me who you are young lady."

Jody was so terrified that she was trembling. She opened her mouth to speak, but no words came out. Finally, she managed to mumble: "I am a very naughty girl who cannot be trusted."

"Don't start that again," implored the Bag Man. Although he looked frightened, too, he whispered to Jody: "Leave this to me. I've been reading a book on being assertive." "Assertive?" Jody asked in a whisper.

"Confident and bold." The Bag Man looked Augustine The Awful straight in the eyes – which meant craning his neck – and said in a calm voice: "There's no problem. We were just walking through the woods and came across this young man."

"Oh, yes," snapped Augustine The Awful, sarcastically through rubbery lips which hardly parted as he spoke in threatening undertones. "You'll be telling me next that you were just passing the time of day with him.

"And I suppose my dogs just happened to take a nap, did they? No, Milo, you don't fool me. You are obviously up to no good."

"So much for your book on assertiveness," Jody said, trying to hide her fear behind a lame joke.

Augustine The Awful now turned his anger on the plump goblin. "I blame you, Bodger, for my dogs being put to sleep. If you had patrolled this area more diligently this would not have happened." "I'm sorry, master," mumbled Bodger, showing a set of badly discoloured, uneven teeth that had not been brushed for a long time. "But I patrol the whole of the land around your castle as well as keeping an eye on these boys for you. As soon as I noticed one of them had stopped work and was talking to intruders I called you on my voice box and suggested you come at once."

"I don't want to listen to excuses," Augustine The Awful told him. "It seems to me, Bodger, you have lived up to your name and bodged things up. Do you know what I did to the last guard who lived up to his name... a fellow called Stinky?"

"Yes, master," Bodger said, bowing his head in shame and dread. "You covered him in gallons of perfume until he drowned."

"Exactly," gloated the wicked wizard. "So be warned! Do you know what I need from you, Bodger, to prevent you suffering a similar fate?"

A desperate Bodger was obviously trying to come up with an answer, but could think of nothing to say. Jody guessed that whatever Augustine required, the wretched goblin wished with all his heart that he could give it to him.

"I need 100 per cent loyalty and obedience. If you fail on either of those counts again you will not be drawing any more wages, Bodger. In fact, you will not be drawing any more breaths."

Bodger gulped and trembled. But Augustine The Awful was no longer paying attention to him. Instead, he stroked his pointed chin as he pondered. "The first thing I need to decide is what to do with the Bag Man and this girl."

"I have a suggestion, master," said Enoch, speaking for the first time.

"Which is?" Augustine The Awful demanded.

"As the Bag Man and the girl have put your dogs to sleep why not turn them into dogs themselves?" Enoch replied, chuckling and revealing teeth even dirtier than those of his fellow guard. "That way their punishment would be appropriate for the crime they committed."

"An excellent idea," Augustine chortled. Delving inside his costume, he produced a large black wand and prepared to cast a spell.

James suddenly intervened. "Couldn't they help us, instead?" he asked, gesturing over to the other two boys who were looking on from their trees.

"Mind your own business, young man," snarled Augustine The Awful. "I'll make the decisions if you don't mind."

He started to wave his wand, but this time Jody interrupted him. "Hold on a moment," she shouted. "It is not us who you should turn into dogs, but your two guards."

"And why would I want to do that?" Augustine The Awful demanded.

"Because they have been plotting to steal from you," Jody said, speaking over a thumping noise, which she suddenly realised was her own heart pounding.

The two guards could hardly believe their ears and cringed with fear. Enoch tried to protest but was overcome by a sneezing fit.

"That's nonsense," insisted Bodger.

"Yes," spluttered Enoch, in between sneezes. "She is just saying that to try to fool you, master. But you are too clever to be fooled by a silly girl."

"Indeed, I am," said Augustine The Awful. "Especially as the girl has already told me she cannot be trusted. Now, young lady, I am about to make you and the Bag Man barking mad."

Jody made one last attempt to convince him. "If I was trying to fool you I wouldn't know what it is you have that they want to steal would I?" she exclaimed.

"So what is it that they want to steal?" said Augustine, now becoming curious.

His eyes were so intense she had to avert her gaze for a split second. But she bravely turned back to face him.

"I heard them saying that you have found the formula for everlasting life. The two main ingredients are in your castle storeroom and when you have mixed all the potions together they intend to steal some of the formula from you. They were talking in the tavern in the town and they didn't know I was there."

Bodger and Enoch were horror struck. But try as they might they could not prevent the guilt showing on their faces, which turned a sickly purple.

Jody seized the initiative. "One of them," she said, nodding towards Enoch, "was waiting to meet a witch to sell her the formula. The witch brought some potions of her own with her, but I knocked her over by accident and broke the tubes she was carrying the potions in. That is why she put a spell on me to make my nose grow and it will continue to get even longer unless I tell everyone I am a very naughty girl who cannot be trusted."

Augustine The Awful was furious. "SO!" he boomed, glaring at the quivering goblins. "You were plotting to steal from me were you? You both need to be punished – and I can't think of anything better than this young lady's suggestion. Instead of you having eternal life you will have a dog's life." He waved his wand and clicked his fingers. Immediately the two goblins disappeared. In their places were two dogs – one with extremely dirty teeth and a mass of unruly fur, and the other plump, with a bald patch on his head. To show Augustine The Awful had a sense of humour, albeit a warped one, the goblins' black boots, now reduced drastically in size, were fitted snugly to the dogs' rear paws.

James and the other two boys, who by now had come down from the tall trees they had climbed to pick berries, looked on open-mouthed in utter astonishment. Jody was also dumbfounded, but she and The Bag Man felt an enormous sense of relief – that it was not them who had been changed into dogs!

Augustine The Awful simply chuckled callously and put his wand away in his costume.

He then addressed a very frightened Bag Man. "Talking of lessons, Milo, obviously you didn't learn yours when I took away your powers. I think I had better lock up you and the girl in my castle until I find out what's going on."

Before Jody could protest Augustine The Awful clapped his hands together twice and muttered a magic phrase.

Immediately Jody and the Bag Man were transported from the woods into a cell in the east tower of the evil wizard's castle.

CHAPTER THIRTEEN

ELSA, the apprentice witch sent by Huffy and Zenda to find Jody and the ingredients for everlasting life, had been flying over the woods on her way to Augustine The Awful's castle when she spotted a group of people gathered below her.

One of them looked remarkably like the evil wizard himself and another seemed to be The Bag Man. There was a boy and a girl there, too – could it be the girl her mistress had described to her?

"Is that the girl my mistress wants?" Elsa said to herself. "Surely I can't be so lucky as to have found her already. I'd better take a closer look, but first I'll make myself invisible." She circled around, chanted the words "zecram, kazam," clapped her hands, and became invisible.

Elsa's eyes lit up with glee as she zoomed down. The closer she got the more certain she became that this was the girl Huffy wanted.

Yes, it was the troublesome Jody, all right. Her shoulder-length hair and long nose confirmed it.

Elsa was about to utter a spell that would send Jody straight to Huffy's cave when the strangest thing happened.

She saw Augustine The Awful clap his hands twice and immediately Jody and The Bag Man, who had been standing next to her, both disappeared.

Elsa, unable to believe her bulging eyes, cursed in frustration. "Damn, damn, damn," she cried out, almost flying into a tree in her fit of rage.

She had to make a sudden change of course to steer her large frame away from the outstretched branches, but could not avoid one of them clipping her ear a painful blow.

As her head cleared, Elsa began to realise what had happened.

Augustine The Awful must have put a spell on the girl and The Bag Man a split second before Elsa could come up with her own spell. 'Just my luck' she thought. 'Never mind. My main task is to find the ingredients for everlasting life in the castle storeroom and take samples of them back to my mistress. I'll do that first and look for the girl later.'

She was still deep in thought when she flew straight into a tree branch.

"Ouch, that hurt" she shrieked.

Continuing her course, Elsa had another thought. 'Perhaps it's time to change myself into the size of a bee. Then I won't keep flying into tree branches'.

But, as an apprentice witch, she wasn't too confident about altering her shape while still invisible and trying to concentrate on her flying. So she made herself visible again before reducing her bulky frame to bee-like proportions. 'Now I can fly through one of the castle windows and then change myself to my normal size when I get inside the storeroom' she thought. 'It won't matter that I'll no longer be invisible. I'll just become my lovely self again.'

It was a decision she was to regret because it was to have tragic consequences.

CHAPTER FOURTEEN

IN Bromley on the fringe of the Kent countryside a distressed Herbert Richards had been searching through James's possessions in a bid to find any clue there might be about his son's disappearance.

He had spent hours looking and it was now well past midnight. But, undeterred at finding nothing, he carried on his search and suddenly spotted a floppy disc that had slipped down the side of the desk in James's bedroom.

The police had already taken away the boy's computer to look through the files, but had apparently missed this floppy disc. Herbert put it in his own computer and began browsing through the large number of items on it.

Finally, he stumbled upon a directory labelled 'Special offers'. One stood out – it was about the Castle of Dreams, offering a free 'adventure holiday of a lifetime'.

Herbert, a gruff, plain speaking accountant who was always suspicious of 'special deals', read his son's notes about the Castle of Dreams with interest and dread.

James had obtained details about this 'free holiday of a lifetime'. There was a questionnaire which James had answered, revealing that he was over 5ft tall, didn't smoke or drink alcohol, was of excellent health and physically fit. He had also been questioned about whether he could climb trees and swim over 10 lengths. James had said he could and had added that he was the freestyle champion in his age group at his local swimming club.

'The police would be very interested in this – it might give them the lead they need,' thought Herbert. 'I'll phone them first thing in the morning.'

But Herbert needed more information to give them. There was only an email address for the Castle of Dreams –- no word of where it was located.

So he sent a message of his own to the Castle of Dreams' email address, asking for more details of the offer. It was a huge mistake because Herbert was merely alerting Augustine The Awful to the fact that someone using James' information pack had traced him.

That night Herbert had no sooner fallen asleep than he was consumed by a terrifying dream. It was the worst nightmare he had ever had, an utterly awful experience that was so vivid it would haunt him all his life.

He found himself in a castle bedroom where he saw James asleep. He tried to wake the boy and urged him to come home with him. But James was in a deep slumber before Herbert could rouse his son he was promptly grabbed from behind by two guards – pixies of contrasting sizes – and coshed by the larger of them.

Herbert was then dragged down a seemingly never-ending series of stone steps into a damp, daunting cell. There he was tied to a large wooden chair by straps that cut into his wrists and ankles, and had a glass of ice-cold water thrown over his face to revive him. He looked up to see the menacing figure of Augustine The Awful towering over him. This time Augustine was dressed in a black gown. But the only things Herbert took in were the evil wizard's tufts of hair, glowering eyes and large pouting lips.

"Now, my friend," said Augustine after introducing himself, his voice low and threatening. "You need to be taught a lesson. Your son logged on to my website of his own free will and signed up to take advantage of my offer of an adventure holiday. Yet you are now trying to get him to break our agreement by enticing him away."

"My son is only 11 years old and you have no right to keep him here," Herbert shouted, struggling in vain against the strapping that bound his wrists to the chair's arms. "I've come to take him home with me – now let us both go. I won't allow you to keep James here."

"Oh, but you will" snapped Augustine. "Furthermore, you'll go home and say nothing because I will erase your memory of this and of what you saw on the disc you found. I have already wiped James's computer clean of his mail to me so nobody will know where he is. But you can be assured that he will be well fed and treated – providing he works hard." "You're mad," snapped Herbert with contempt. He had hardly got the words out than he felt a stinging slap across the face from the back of Augustine's right hand. The ring the wizard was wearing cut into his flesh.

"Don't you dare insult me," Augustine hissed. "If I have any more trouble from you I'll have to move James from his nice, comfortable room to this cell with some friends of mine. The sort of friends he won't like.

"Let me introduce them to you." He turned to one of the guards and ordered: "Pass me the boxes containing my pets."

"Yes, master," said the smaller guard, picking up six of the 12 wooden boxes he had brought into the cell earlier and left on the floor behind him. He passed the first box to Augustine.

"These boxes contain my collection of spiders and scorpions," purred the evil wizard gleefully. "Now what have we here?" He inspected the box and then answered his own question: "Ah, it's Trevor. He's a tarantula. Let me show you."

He opened the lid of the box and placed it on the lap of a trembling Herbert, who watched in horror as two large spider's legs emerged from the front of the box, followed quickly by others.

Herbert's screams did not deter the two-inch hairy tarantula crawling out on to his heaving stomach, which was covered only by his shirt, and making its way cautiously towards his chest.

The spider's eight eyes, the middle two of which stood out from its triangular head, seemed to be focused on Herbert's face and its jaws opened in anticipation of food.

"Would you like to see another?" asked Augustine The Awful, as a second box was passed to him. "This one is called Roxanne and she's a red-back. Just one bite from her and you'll be in no state to attend to any demands Mrs. Richards may make of you. You'll be in excruciating pain, sweating all over and vomiting like mad."

He opened the lid slightly and pushed the box towards his victim so that the red-back's eight long spindly legs could be seen making frantic movements in a bid to get free. A reddish-orange stripe down its back was plainly visible. "No, no. Take it away from me," shrieked a near demented Herbert, sweat dripping from his forehead and receding hair line.

"I take it she's not your type," taunted Augustine, putting Roxanne's box to one side. "It's just as well because she has this nasty habit of eating her partner after mating and spinning up to eight round balls of web containing hundreds of eggs. Never mind, I've plenty of others. How about Bobby the black widow?"

Herbert screamed again and started to shake uncontrollably. "No?" queried Augustine. "Well, there's Michael the mantid or Hector the huntsman." He peered into another box. "Hector, like most of his family, comes from the tropics – I had him shipped over from the Caribbean. If he sinks his fangs into you you'll suffer swelling, sickness, headaches and maybe palpitations.

"Oh, how disappointing. It looks as if Hector is asleep. He wouldn't be in the mood for running about."

As he spoke the tarantula continued to make slow but deliberate progress up Herbert's chest within inches of his mouth which was now emitting bile as he retched in disgust. "I know," said Augustine, a sparkle coming briefly into the deep pools of black that were his eyes. "You and the tarantula would find it simply riveting to meet Ralph my red scorpion."

Augustine The Awful opened a large box containing the red scorpion and tipped it upside down so that a reddish-brown creature measuring a full seven inches fell on Herbert's lap. It's abdomen plopped against Herbert's shirt, which was now covered in sweat.

The scorpion raised itself on its eight stringy legs. Ralph's upwardly curved tail – arched threateningly over its back, ready to sting – moved sharply from side to side in an agitated manner as it spotted the tarantula.

The tarantula stopped in its tracks and turned to face the scorpion, which was opening its two lobster-like claws in anticipation.

"When the scorpion captures a victim with its claws it inflicts a disabling string with its tail," Augustine The Awful explained, grinning fiendishly. "The problem for you is that you are shaking so much you are upsetting Ralph even more than Trevor is. And Trevor doesn't look very happy, either. I hope Ralph doesn't bite you because he's a special breed and can be deadly."

Every nerve in Herbert's body was on end as he tried to stop himself making a violent movement that would cause the two potential combatants to join forces in attacking him. "It will be interesting to see whether one of them bites you first or each other," mused Augustine. "Perhaps I should give them something to whet their appetites."

With that, he took a jar from one of the pockets of his gown and held it in front of Herbert for him to see. It contained hundreds of smaller spiders all crawling over each other as they frantically tried to get out of their glass cage. "These are not poisonous but they crawl literally everywhere," said Augustine as he slowly opened the top of the jar and shook it so that the spiders tumbled out on to Herbert's chest, some falling on to his skin where the top two buttons of his shirt were undone.

Herbert screamed hysterically but the wizard ignored his cries.

"They are frisky little fellows aren't they?" he said. "Look at them. They're running in all directions. Some down your chest towards your stomach and others towards your mouth. I'm sure no matter how tightly you close it that they'll find a way in. Or maybe they will prefer to go up your nose and..."

Herbert let out three more ear-piecing shrieks before he finally passed out.

When Herbert awoke the spiders were gone. He blinked in disbelief at finding himself at home in his own bed and not in Augustine The Awful's castle. But Herbert's feeling of immense relief could not compensate for the state of shock he was still in.

He lay on the bed trembling and perspiring as his wife Marjorie wiped his forehead and arms to get rid of the sweat which had made the sheets quite damp.

"Thank goodness you've woken up at last," his wife said, soothingly. "You've obviously had a dreadful nightmare." "Yes," he muttered. "It was about spiders. They were crawling all over me."

Marjorie's lightly freckled face grimaced in disgust. "How awful," she said.

Herbert was on the point of telling her about the wicked wizard. But then his mind went blank and he remembered nothing of Augustine The Awful, the castle – or the computer disc. Nor could he explain the cut on his cheek. But the shock to his nervous system left other unseen scars and a lifelong fear of spiders.

CHAPTER FIFTEEN

JODY'S shock at finding herself in a cell in the bleak east tower of Augustine The Awful's castle was matched by her disgust at sharing such a confined space with several beetles and two rats.

The stone walls and floors of the small room were completely bare, apart from a bed covered by a single sheet on which the Bag Man had placed his carrier bags. He had already inspected the cell door, made of solid oak, which was securely locked, and found that the only 'window' was a narrow slit in the stone wall on the right, above the bed. By climbing on to the old fashioned wooden bed frame he could peer through the slit and see a sheer drop to the moat that surrounded the castle four floors below.

"I suppose there's no chance of escaping," Jody sighed, flopping dejectedly on to the edge of the bed.

"It would appear not," the Bag Man agreed.

"When Augustine The Awful comes I'll tell him James is my brother and demand he sets all three of us free," she said defiantly.

"I don't think that would be a good idea," the Bag Man advised. "If Augustine The Awful has wiped out James's memory and tricked him into working in the forest then he will hardly want to release him. And should the evil-minded Augustine find out you are James's sister he'll never let you go. But I doubt if he would release us anyway, now that you know he has found the formula for everlasting life."

"What can we do, then?"

The Bag Man shrugged. "We can't do anything at the moment. We'll just have to wait."

The wait proved to be a very long one as several hours passed without a sound, apart from the two large rats scurrying across the stone floor and water dripping from a leak in one corner of the ceiling, which housed a family of cockroaches. Jody, overcome by morbid fascination, watched them moving from one crevice to another.

It was getting dark in the small, smelly cell because even a full moon could not throw much light through the narrow slit of a window.

Finally, they heard a noise of approaching footsteps and the cell door was unlocked by two pixies, dressed in dark blue uniforms and pointed hats. They were the direct opposites of each other. One was large and the other comparatively small.

The large pixie had rugged features, with a scar running down his otherwise unmarked face. The small pixie was spotty, with a bent nose and a squint. He seemed to have something in his mouth that caused him to chew and squint alternatively. In fact, the chewing and squinting were just nervous habits.

"I am a very naughty girl who cannot be trusted," Jody told them. The pixies looked at each other and then at Jody as if she was deranged. But they quickly pushed the heavy wooden cell door wide open to allow some light to flood into the gap – and Augustine The Awful to enter. He brought with him an aura of evil just like his brother Hugo, and the very sight of him made Jody's flesh crawl.

"WELL," bellowed Augustine The Awful menacingly, through his rubbery lips as he strutted into the cell in his usual arrogant manner. "Are you now prepared to tell me the true purpose of your visit to the woods?"

"We've done nothing wrong," cried Jody, jumping off the bed on which she and the Bag Man had been sitting. "You've told me lies for a start," Augustine The Awful roared back at her, huffing and puffing, which caused his chest to rise and fall sharply with each intake of breath.

"What lies?" the Bag Man inquired, getting off the edge of the bed and rising to his feet.

Augustine The Awful looked at him with scorn. "You told me you just happened to be walking in the woods. So it may interest you to know that when my brother Hugo Toby telephoned to arrange to visit me tomorrow he informed me that a girl with long brownish hair, just like this one, visited his house looking for her brother James.

"Do you still claim you just happened to come across the boy by accident?"

"All right, I was looking for him," Jody admitted, defiantly.

"And he is my brother. I've come to take him home."

"Have you now?" Augustine The Awful mocked, a vile smile spreading across his shallow cheeks and swollen lips. "Presumably you are unaware your father has seen for himself that your brother is being well treated here?" "That's not true," shouted Jody.

"Enough!" ordered Augustine The Awful, holding up his hand. "I think the time has come to put an end to your rudeness by silencing you for good." He rolled up his sleeves menacingly.

"Leave her alone!" challenged the Bag Man, moving towards his old foe.

"Is this you being assertive again?" taunted the evil wizard. "Yes, it is," snapped Milo. "And I can be threatening, too." He clenched his fists and raised them.

The two pixies stepped forward to protect their master, though the smaller of the two, still chewing and squinting, was content to let his colleague take the initiative. But Augustine The Awful was in command of the situation. "It's all right, Olaf," he told the larger pixie. "Seeing you and little Grog inflict some pain on Milo would give me great pleasure, but I think he needs to be taught a more subtle lesson." The Bag Man swung a blow at his old foe, who ducked to avoid it. With that Augustine The Awful clicked his fingers and uttered a curse. There was a puff of smoke and the Bag Man vanished.

A croaking sound was coming from where he had been standing, and Jody looked down in horror to see that in the Bag Man's place was a very mournful-looking frog. "That's better," said Augustine The Awful, sneering. "Now I have changed you into a frog you look much less assertive, though I must say more appealing." He turned to Jody. "As for you, a night in this cell with a frog will teach you a lesson. Then I'll decide what to do with you. You look quite a strong girl, are you any good at chopping trees and swimming?"

But Jody wasn't listening to him. She shrieked: "Look what you've done to the Bag Man. You horrid, horrid wizard. Change him back immediately."

The frog croaked in agreement.

"Don't you dare tell me what to do," bellowed Augustine The Awful, enraged at the girl's insolent remarks. "I'll never change him back – he will be a frog until the day he dies – or in his case until he croaks for the last time." He laughed at his own cruel joke.

"Why are you doing this to us and why have you got my brother working for you?" questioned Jody, her blue eyes flashing angrily at him.

"I needed your brother and those other two boys to climb those giant trees for me and collect the golden berries from them because, apart from Olaf here, none of the other pixies or goblins are any good at climbing. They kept falling off the trees long before they got to the top. After all, those Golden Berry trees are the tallest in the world.

"Boys love climbing trees so it was no problem for them. The fact that your brother and the other two are good swimmers has proved helpful as well because I also need plant life from the river-bed.

"That has left Olaf and Grog free to attend to other important tasks. Isn't that right, Grog?" He turned to the smaller pixie who nodded his head, too scared to open his mouth in case the wrong words came out. Grog actually stopped chewing but carried on squinting.

"So I recruited boys young enough to do as they were told, but old enough and big enough to work hard."

"But why do you want the boys to climb trees for golden berries?"

"I suppose there's no harm in telling you," the wizard mused. "The juice from the berries is one of the main ingredients those two treacherous goblins wanted to steal from me. By getting Olaf and Grog to extract the juice and mix it with a secret compound from the river-bed as well as my own special potion I have produced the powerful formula that will stop me from ageing.

"I had to try out hundreds of different compounds before I finally hit upon the right formula for ever- lasting life. I have tested it on a guinea pig, which has not aged at all.

"Now I simply need to get some more plant life from the bottom of the river and keep mixing it with the berry juice and my own special potion.

"Once it is refined I can drink it regularly and will be able to live for ever, building up my riches and increasing my power until I rule the whole world. It won't take much longer." "Does that mean you will let James go?"

"No it doesn't," snapped the wizard. "The formula has to be taken every week so there will be a lot more trees for your brother and the other boys to climb. And when they are not climbing for the berries they will be plucking more plant life from the river-bed."

"But James can't stay here. He has to go back to school and lead his own life," Jody insisted. "He should never have come here at all."

It seemed Augustine The Awful was going to ignore the girl's impertinence, but he couldn't resist telling her how clever he was to lure James to his castle.

In making the effort to honour her with an answer, as if even speaking was too much trouble for him, Augustine The Awful slowly parted his puffy lips so narrowly that his voice sounded even more sinister than usual.

He hissed: "As I told your father, James came here of his own accord. I sent out an advertisement from my computer website, inviting boys to come to the Castle of Dreams for a free holiday – and climb as many trees as they liked. Lots of boys answered by filling in my questionnaire. I chose James and the other two boys because they best met my requirements so I transported them here.

"James wanted to return home to tell his parents about the adventure holiday I was offering him, but I persuaded him that it was first necessary for him to sign a short work placement agreement to pay his way."

"How short?" Jody demanded to know.

"I believe the figure 25 was mentioned," Augustine The Awful recalled.

"Months?" Jody queried.

"Years", he sniggered. "The small print on the back of the consent form also said that if the boys don't stick to the agreement there is a penalty clause under which I can turn them into goblins."

"You wicked, wicked man," Jody screamed. "You tricked James and then you wiped out his memory, didn't you?"

"I thought that would be for the best," Augustine The Awful confided. "I'm sure your father would rather not have any memory of his brief encounter with me – after all, it gave him the biggest nightmare of his life."

"What do you mean?" Jody demanded.

Augustine mocked her with a shame-face expression as he revealed: "Your father looked on James' computer disc and found that he had replied to my website. So I thought I had better bring your dad here to straighten things out. I taught him a lesson with the help of my friends Trevor, Roxanne, Michael, Hector and Ralph."

"Who are they?" she asked.

"They are my collection of spiders and scorpions. They loved your father so much some of them crawled all over him."

"You loathsome man," Jody shouted, revolted.

"Such anger," Augustine taunted. "I think it would be best if I wiped out your memory as well as that of your brother's and father's. But I'll sleep on it and decide what to do with you tomorrow. I must go now – I hope you and the frog have sweet dreams."With that he marched out of the cell door, which the two pixies slammed shut behind him and bolted from the outside.

Jody looked across at the frog, who was sitting silently on the stone floor. "Oh, you poor Bag Man – I mean Milo," she said.

"I'm so sorry you've been turned into a frog – it's all my fault for getting you into this." Milo croaked in reply to show he understood.

She suddenly noticed for the first time that the pixies had left some food and water to one side of the large oak door. She shared it with the frog who then made himself as comfortable as he could in a corner of the cell.

Jody climbed on to the bed and pulled the sheet over her, causing two of the carrier bags to fall on the floor. But the sheet hardly helped to keep out the bitter wind blowing from the window slit in the wall, and a torn, coarse mattress, which had lost much of its stuffing, offered no warmth, either.

The only comfort for the frightened girl as darkness filled the primitive cell was that the rats and insects had slunk away, presumably to go to sleep.

Eventually Jody shut her eyes in an attempt to get some sleep herself. She was too cold and too scared to do so, however. Instead, she opened her eyes again and stared into the darkness, longing to be in the warm arms of her mother.

Faces came floating into her mind – her mother's, smiling lovingly; her father's, looking strained and bothered; Hugo Toby's mean piercing eyes staring down his long nose; Wiffle's broad grin through his flowing white beard; Augustine The Awful's evil scowl and rubbery lips; and finally Milo's startled expression before being turned into a frog.

The images disturbed her so much she lay awake for hours, her sobs only interrupted by her teeth chattering in the dark, damp atmosphere. Finally, her head fell back on to the single, grubby pillow and she drifted into a disturbed but welcome sleep.

CHAPTER SIXTEEN

JODY awoke with a start the next morning in the half-light, drowsily thinking she was at home and wondering why her mother had not called her to get ready for school.

She peered into the gloom of the cell to get her bearings and looked down from her bed to see what appeared to be a rat scurrying across the stone floor. Then the cold realisation hit her that she was locked up in Augustine The Awful's castle. To make matters worse her nose was half an inch longer and the unfortunate Bag Man was now a frog! The distressed girl saw the frog was no longer sitting in the corner, but had hopped across the stone floor to the end of her bed where two of the carrier bags had fallen. His head was inside one of the bags and he seemed to be looking at a book.

"What is it?" asked Jody. "Is that something important?" The frog turned to face her and screeched: "Redit, redit."

"I know you've read it," she said, smiling. "But is it something I should know about?"

The frog croaked in agreement.

So Jody jumped out of bed, walked over to the carrier bag and took out the book. It had a battered cardboard cover, the corners of which were bent, and was entitled 'Spells And How To Use Them'.

She looked at the page the frog had open and began to read it.

At first she could not comprehend what the frog was referring to. Then her eyes fell on a passage that said: 'If a wizard grants you a wish you can use it for anything that is positive. You cannot normally harm anyone with the wish. But should someone cast an evil spell you can use the wish to reverse the spell and turn it against the person who cast it.'

"Do you mean I could use my wish which Wiffle granted me to reverse Augustine The Awful's spell?" she questioned, pushing her long hair back as it threatened to fall across her face. "Would that enable me to turn you back into your true self and turn Augustine The Awful into a frog?"

The frog's eyes lit up with pleasure as it croaked excitedly. "But it also means I would no longer have a wish to take James and I home, and we would be stuck here," she said ruefully.

The frog seemed to visibly shrink and dropped his eyes mournfully.

"Don't fret, Milo," she comforted him. "I'll do it. I owe you that. Without you, I'd never have found James. But what must I do?"

"Redit, redit," cried the frog, excitedly.

Jody looked back at the book and scanned the page. She read out loud: 'In order to use a wish to turn an evil spell against a wizard or a witch there is one proviso. 'The offending wizard or witch must agree that the spell they cast was a wicked one. Otherwise the matter must go before a panel of wizards for a ruling.'

"How ridiculous," she snapped. "A wizard who has made an evil spell would hardly be stupid enough to admit it was wicked, would he? And we don't happen to have a panel of wizards to call on. It's simply impossible."

At that moment there was the sound of footsteps and the bolts on the big oak door were pulled back by the two pixie guards, Olaf and Grog.

They put down bowls of food and drink and then promptly left, locking the door firmly behind them. It was not until long after the girl and the frog had eaten that the guards returned and this time opened the cell door wide so that Augustine The Awful could enter.

Once again Augustine The Awful towered over them all. Jody would have been shaking with fright if it had not been for the fact the nasty wizard was now dressed all in red instead of the more menacing black. But, without his brother's pot belly, he was no figure of fun and was still a disturbing sight. "Good morning!" he greeted them. He turned to address Jody: "I trust you and the frog both slept well. I've decided what to do with you, young lady. I'm going to let you work in the forest with your brother and the other two boys. First, I'm going to wipe out your memory so you don't go disturbing the boys."

Jody thought quickly. "Can't I work with you as your assistant instead?" she asked. "I could help you keep notes about your formula for everlasting life and file all your papers." Her big blue eyes looked at him appealingly.

"I've already written up my notes," grunted Augustine The Awful. "But just why would you want to be my assistant?" he asked, very suspiciously, stroking his pointed chin.

"I could learn so much from you," Jody explained. "You're wicked."

"Don't call me names!" he reprimanded her.

"No, you misunderstand," she explained, forcing a wide smile she hoped was all sweetness and light.

"We sometimes use the term 'wicked' to mean 'terrific'. You obviously have never seen Ali G on television or at the cinema."

"I don't know who this Ali G is," Augustine The Awful told her. "But if he says 'wicked' means 'terrific' I like him." "Well," she cooed at him. "It wasn't very nice of you to turn the Bag Man into a frog, but it was a terrific trick. And that's what Ali G would call 'wicked'."

"Yes," agreed Augustine The Awful, smiling with pride. "It was . 'wicked'."

This was what she had been praying he would say. She now plucked up every ounce of her courage and, staring into his menacing eyes, she told him: "As you have confessed it was wicked, I now wish that your spell be reversed and that you become a frog instead of the Bag Man."

A look of rage spread over Augustine's face, giving way to one of horror. "So you've tried to trick me, have you ..." he shouted. "I'll teach you ...."

Jody feared the worst. But Augustine The Awful never finished his sentence.

Instead, the huge wizard suddenly disappeared and was replaced by a small slimy, bloated frog.

Jody turned round to look at the other frog, but it was no longer there. It had been replaced by the beaming figure of the Bag Man, returned to his true self.

"Thank you," he said. "I can't thank you enough."

She rushed up and embraced him. As the Bag Man hugged her back, he could see the bigger of the two pixies, Olaf, moving menacingly towards them. The smaller one, his crooked nose twitching and beady eyes squinting, looked almost as threatening as he followed Olaf's lead.

The Bag Man slipped out of Jody's arms and held out his hand to stop them. "I wouldn't try anything foolish," he warned them. "Now that I have switched places with Augustine The Awful doesn't it occur to you that I may have inherited his powers?"

The pixies stopped dead in their tracks and looked at him questioningly. "I don't think so," said Olaf, taking another step forward.

"You're bluffing," Grog taunted. But he squinted and chewed nervously.

"Do you want me to prove my powers?" asked Milo. Before they could answer he chanted a spell, clicked his thumbs against his fingers and suddenly water gushed all over the pixies' heads as if they were caught under a heavy shower. "Are you satisfied – or do you think I should do something far worse?" he demanded.

"No, no," Grog cried out, as the water dripped from him.

"Please make it stop."

The Bag Man clapped his hands and the shower ended as abruptly as it had started.

"That was brilliant," said Jody in admiration.

"Yes, it was quite good:" said Milo in false modesty. "Well, gentleman, are you now convinced about my powers. Or would you like a further demonstration?"

"We believe you," muttered Olaf, ringing water from his mass of black hair.

"In that case, gentlemen, would you please take the frog and throw him out of the cell window into the moat that runs around the castle. That will wipe out his memory and he will never order you around again."

Olaf and Grog looked at the frog and then at each other warily.

"Wouldn't you like to be rid of a heartless master?" asked Milo.

"Indeed, we would," said Olaf, moving forward purposefully. The frog jumped frantically away and managed to escape the clutches of the pursuing pixies. But Olaf and Grog chased after it and finally, following three abortive attempts, succeeded in cornering it.

They managed to lift the struggling creature off the floor between them and then climbed on to the bed in order to reach the 'window'.

Finding they were not tall enough, Olaf took the frog in both hands and stood unsteadily on Grog's back. The frog cried out in rage and frustration, and finally in pain as Olaf, stretching his arms above his head, forced it through the slit in the wall.

One final push caused it to drop down into the water beneath.

A loud splattering sound came from the moat outside, followed by a 'plop', as the frog hit the water – after first bouncing off the side of the castle wall!

"Uga Oooo," shouted the Bag Man in mock pain.

Then he turned to the two pixies. "Thank you, gentleman," he said. "You should be very pleased with yourselves in ridding us all of such a terrible ogre. Now perhaps you would be good enough to tell us where the three boys are." "They are already in the forest working," replied Olaf, still dripping wet.

"Then lead the way out of here," instructed the Bag Man.

CHAPTER SEVENTEEN

THE Bag Man picked up his carrier bags, stuffed his book on spells into one of them, and ushered the two pixies and Jody out of the open cell door.

As they marched down the cobbled corridor Jody told him: "You were wonderful. I didn't know when I reversed that spell that you would inherit Augustine The Awful's powers. Now you can send James and I back home."

He stopped her and whispered in her ear. "I haven't and I can't."

"What do you mean?" Jody asked, puzzled.

"I haven't got any new powers and therefore I can't send you home. I only made out that I had inherited Augustine's powers to fool the two pixies. I still can't work any special magic unfortunately."

"But you made that water fall on their heads," Jody pointed out.

"Shush, or they'll hear you," warned the Bag Man. "If you remember I told you that after Augustine The Awful took away my special powers I was left with only a couple of basic magic tricks to cater for everyday needs. One was to conjure up food and drink and the other was to produce rain-water.

"So I made loads of rain gush down on the pixies' heads . I usually use that trick to do simple things such as water plants.

"Unfortunately, I can't do anything spectacular like transport anyone or send you and James back home."

"Oh," sighed Jody. "Then how will we ever get back to England?"

"We'll worry about that later," said the Bag Man. "First, we've got to find your brother and those other boys and persuade them to come with us. You heard Augustine The Awful say that his brother Hugo is coming here to visit him today, and we can't afford to let him discover us." He put his carrier bags in one hand and took Jody's arm in an effort to propel her towards the pixies, who were leaving a trail of water behind them.

"But shouldn't we search for the notes that Augustine The Awful said he has kept on his formula for eternal life?" Jody protested.

"We haven't got time," the Bag Man said. "He could have hidden them anywhere."

"At the very least we should go to the storeroom and destroy the main ingredients for the formula," Jody insisted. "If we don't it will be easy for Hugo Toby or the witch to find them. Then they could uncover the secret of eternal life and use it for evil purposes."

"I suppose you are right," sighed the Bag Man. "But we must hurry – we can't risk Hugo Toby arriving and catching us here."

He strode after the fast disappearing pixies.

"Slow down, fellows" he called to them. The pixies came to a halt.

"Do you know when Augustine The Awful's brother will be arriving?" the Bag Man asked them.

"No," they chorused.

"Well," said the Bag Man. "He will be coming soon and when he does I suggest that it will be in your interests not to tell him that his brother has been turned into a frog. Just say that Augustine The Awful left in a hurry and didn't mention where he was going. Now I think Grog should go and prepare for Hugo's arrival, while Olaf takes us to the storeroom before we find the boys."

"But the storeroom will be guarded," Olaf pointed out. "We'll take our chances," the Bag Man told him.

The storeroom was near the top of the castle's west tower, which meant climbing up flight upon flight of stone steps on a very narrow stairway. When they got to the corridor leading to the storeroom's solid oak door it was deserted. "I can't understand it," said Olaf. "The master told me that the storeroom was to be guarded, but there is nobody here." The Bag Man ignored him and tried to open the heavy oak door, only to find it securely locked.

"Now what?" asked Jody, shaking the wrought iron handle herself without causing it to budge an inch. "There's no way we can get in, is there?"

"That remark is going into the book in black ink, young lady," said the Bag Man, winking at her. "Please try to have more faith in me." He rummaged in his carrier bags and, after a couple of unsuccessful fumblings, he pulled out a huge set of skeleton keys.

The Bag Man patiently tried them one by one in the lock. After the tenth key had failed to turn Olaf and Jody began to get agitated.

"Why don't you just use your magic powers to make the door open?" suggested Olaf. "That would be much easier." "Magic should be used sparingly," the Bag Man replied, trying not to show any alarm. "Just have some patience." He tried three more keys, none of which fitted properly, and there were now only three left. But, just as all seemed lost, the next key slipped into the lock and turned smoothly.

The Bag Man threw the door open to reveal a huge stone room in the far corner of which were six barrels.

But as they approached them a bellow of dark smoke appeared, causing them to jump back.

Out of the foul-smelling haze sprang an horrendous looking monster, which resembled an upright double-length dragon with an elongated neck and hideous head on the top of which were two huge horns.

It was covered mainly with large scales, though there were a few patches of matted hair. What were most noticeable were it's blazing, bloodshot red and yellow eyes and sharp fangs that shot out from slime-covered gums.

If that was not bad enough, it had terrible claws which looked capable of ripping anything to bits. The creature suddenly opened its massive mouth to emit a short burst of flame, forcing the terrified trio to cower against the door.

"Who are you and what do you want?" the thing demanded in a booming voice full of menace.

Jody's blue eyes opened even wider than usual as she stood rooted to the spot with fear. But she managed to stammer: "My name is Jody. I am a very naughty girl who cannot be trusted. But who...who are you?"

"I'm the Monster from Hell. I have been created by Augustine The Awful to guard these barrels," the monster informed them. "And if anyone comes near them I am to kill them." With that it opened its mouth to send a second, bigger flash of fire across the room, as if to demonstrate its power.

"How would you like some food?" asked the Bag Man, thinking he could doctor it with a drug and send the creature off to sleep. "I can provide you with some juicy steaks."

"I don't need any steaks," came the reply. "I've been suffering from indigestion after eating a young but very ugly witch. I'm not sure how she got in here, but she suddenly appeared. She began trying to remove some of the contents from these barrels which the master asked me to guard." "Did the witch cast a spell on you?" asked Olaf, unable to believe that his master could have created something quite as dreadful as this.

"No she didn't. I caught her opening one of the barrels and she seemed absolutely flabbergasted when she saw me," chortled the monster. "She was so shocked she dropped her wand as she tried to get it out.

"Unfortunately I didn't have enough time to decide whether I was going to roast her or grill her. As it was, I burnt her young flesh to a crisp. It was a shame because even her giblets were over-done.

"But I washed her down with 16 slugs and a very tasty rat. I would have preferred a frog, but maybe I could find room in my stomach for you three instead once this indigestion goes. I could take more time cooking you. The girl would be nice toasted. I could cook you three now and eat you later." The Bag Man frantically looked through his carrier bags to see if he could find something to stop the monster as it took one step towards them. "Yes, I think I could soon manage another course," it said, licking its large tongue. "You three would do nicely."

"Do something," urged Olaf. "Use your magic powers." Milo clicked his thumbs against his fingers as the creature was about to throw out another burst of flame from its ghastly mouth and a heavy shower of water fell to extinguish it. "Now it's time to use your assertiveness" Jody said encouragingly, as the 'thing' looked dumbstruck.

"I'll give it a try," the Bag Man agreed "Perhaps I should resort to the 'stiff upper lip technique' I've been reading about." He raised his voice to address the monster in a superior upper crust accent. "You don't seem to understand the situation, my dear fellow. We have just come from Augustine The Awful."

As Milo spoke he delved into one of his bags and brought out two packets. "I have something for you, and in view of the fact you enjoy eating frogs I know Augustine The Awful wants you to have it right away."

"What is it?" demanded the beast. But it watched transfixed as the Bag Man took a syringe from one packet and a small glass vessel from the other. Milo then calmly uncapped the needle of the syringe and drew half the liquid from the vessel.

"It's time to use the 'doctor-patient technique'," he whispered to Jody. "This is just part of the castle's health and hygiene procedures," he informed the 'thing'. "Presumably Augustine The Awful has told you about health and hygiene procedures."

"No he hasn't," growled the creature, its bulging eyes blazing in annoyance.

"Well, they have to be followed," the Bag Man assured it. "Now roll up your sleeve – ah, of course, you haven't got one."

"Don't come near me with that," warned the monster. "Don't be such a baby," the Bag Man told him. "I'm not going to hurt you."

"I said NO!" bellowed the monster and shoved out its huge tongue to whip the vessel out of the Bag Man's hands. But, in doing so, it caused the remainder of the liquid to gush out into its mouth. Within seconds the monster was gasping and, after letting out an anguished cry, it collapsed dramatically in a heap on the floor unconscious.

"Well, I never," said the Bag Man. "It's done the job for me by self administering the dose."

"That was very brave of you and so assertive," cried a relieved Jody, hugging him. "But I don't think the monster would ever have allowed you to get near enough to use that needle."

"Maybe not," admitted the Bag Man. "Though it is amazing what you can get away with as long as you remain calm and self assured. As my book says, it's just a matter of having the confidence to carry it off."

"What was in that bottle?" asked Olaf.

"It's what you would call a magic potion," the Bag Man answered. "It's actually a drug containing the slime from a frog, the tail of a rat and the sting of a bee."

"But that wouldn't knock the creature out cold like that," Jody insisted, wrapping her arms around herself to keep out the chill of the damp storeroom.

"Ah, I forgot," said the Bag Man, reading the label on the back of the bottle that was still in his hand. "It also contained, in equal measures, the poisons of a snake, a deadly spider and a scorpion."

"That would be enough to knock it out," Jody agreed. "You might have even killed it."

"No, it's still alive – I can hear it breathing," volunteered Olaf, moving forward cautiously.

Taking care to walk around the prostrate monster, Jody and the Bag Man went over to the six barrels in the corner and lifted the lids to reveal the juice from the golden berries in five of them and something that smelt like river plants in the other.

"How can we destroy the ingredients?" Jody asked.

"The witches are already trying to get their hands on them."

"Let me see if I have something in my bags," the Bag Man answered. He searched the first, pulling out a pair of old smelly socks, a bar of chocolate and a coat hanger. But after delving into the second bag he eventually came across a tube of super glue. "This should do the trick," he said. "It is a special glue that will set any chemical rock hard. So nobody will be able to use what is in the barrels."

But try as he might he could not get any out of the tube. "Damn," he said. "It seems to have come into contact with some of the orange drink I keep in the bag and has set itself solid."

"That wasn't very clever was it?" scolded Jody, putting her hands deep into her dress pockets to keep them warm. "You're in the black book again," the Bag Man rebuked her. We'll just have to find something else."

"How about this?" Jody asked, yanking something out of one of her pockets. It was the sachets she had obtained at the café which turned out to be a petrol station.

She read the label on one of the sachets: "It says 'Zingers – the special acid drops that put a zing under your car bonnet and

burn away any rust. Extra strong. Do not touch or drink.'
Nobody is going to be able to drink what's in the barrels if we
put this acid in it are they?"

"Ideal," agreed the Bag Man. "The acid would burn
anyone's lips as soon as it touched them."

He helped Jody break open the sachets and tip some of the
contents into each of the six barrels, taking care not to touch the
acid. Then, turning to the pixie, he asked: "Do you know where
your master kept the other secret ingredients, Olaf?"

"He never let me see them," Olaf replied, rubbing the scar
on his face ruefully. "I don't even know what they are." "What
about the formula? Augustine The Awful must have kept
notes," Jody persisted.

"Perhaps they are in his study or his lounge, I don't know."
"Why don't we..." but Jody was cut short by the Bag Man. "We
haven't time to look," he insisted. "Augustine The Awful's
brother will be here soon. We must go to the forest now and
find the boys."

"I'll take you out of the castle and get you past the guards on
the front entrance," Olaf offered. "But when we reach the spot
where the boys are working in the forest you had better use
your magic powers to stop the dogs attacking you." The Bag
Man smiled as he picked up his bags, stepped round the
monster and headed for the door. "That's one trick I'll be happy
to do. It looks like the dogs will be tucking into some nice juicy
steaks again."

CHAPTER EIGHTEEN

ZENDA hated leaving her luxury quarters to go into her mother's barren cavern but it was necessary to talk to the old bat.

"What's wrong, dear," Huffy Haggard greeted her daughter. "I'm a little concerned that Elsa has not reported back," Zenda admitted. "Perhaps, on reflection, I placed too much trust in her."

"Yes, it is strange she has not returned. But maybe it is taking her longer than we thought to find where the secret potion is stored."

Zenda made a 'V' shape with her long fingers, and saw to her disgust that the black varnish on one of nails had flaked off. She tutted at what was her second cause for annoyance. "Perhaps I should send one of our eagles to fly over the castle and investigate," she mused.

"Well, we don't want to raise any suspicions at the castle by having a two-headed eagle hovering around there, do we dear?" Huffy pointed out. "If Augustine The Awful spots it, he will guess that we have sent it.

"We could wait a little longer to see if either Elsa or those two goblins I spoke to come up trumps."

"Maybe, you're right," Zenda conceded. "But it won't do any harm to send a bird to look in the town and the forest for that troublesome girl Jody, will it?"

"But if one of our eagles finds her, can it be trusted to bring the girl back to us?" Huffy queried. "It might kill her."

"So?" asked Zenda, rubbing the offending fingernail. "That wouldn't be a problem, would it?"

CHAPTER NINETEEN

TRUE to his word, Olaf took Jody and The Bag Man out through the front gate of the castle past the guards – two ugly goblins.

As the trio made their way to the forest, Olaf warned: "Make sure you don't get trapped by one of the creepers."

"What are they?" asked Jody.

"They are long pink plants which grow among the grass and can wrap themselves around you," Olaf replied. "Some of them are so strong they can do you a serious injury and even crush you to death.

"Before Augustine recruited your brother and the other two boys, he created a giant pixie to pick golden berries for him. But the pixie was slow and stupid and lazy. He stopped working early one day and while wandering through the forest he lay down and fell asleep. When he woke up he was trapped by the creepers.

"They were so big they had wrapped themselves completely around him."

"What happened to him?" Jody inquired rather apprehensively. "Did the creeper kill him?"

"Not quite – but Augustine did when he found him," Olaf told her. "He said that fools were no use to him. Augustine is absolutely ruthless and if he ever escapes from the spell you put on him he will kill us all – you can be sure of that." "Don't worry," said The Bag Man soothingly. "How can he possibly escape? He will remain a frog for the rest of his life."

From then on Jody and The Bag Man kept their eyes pinned to the ground looking for creepers until a giant bird circled overhead.

"That's a strange bird," said Jody, looking up alarmed as it drew nearer. "It looks as if it has got two heads."

"It has," The Bag Man confirmed. "It could be one of the witches' eagles." Suddenly the eagle swooped down towards Jody.

The startled girl tried to scamper away, only to trip on a creeper.

"Look out" shouted Olaf, but the warning was too late.

A frantic Jody screamed for help as the plant's long stalk wrapped itself around her ankle, causing her to crash to the ground.

The fall proved to be a blessing because it took her beyond the eagle's swoop.

Milo acted with amazing speed for a man who had seemed so ponderous. He raced over to a burrow, pushed his arm deep into it and yanked out a rabbit, just like a magician pulling one of the furry animals from a hat.

As the eagle prepared to attack Jody, Milo threw the rabbit at it. The eagle's natural instinct took over and it sunk its talons into the terrified bunny which shrieked like a banshee. Olaf was equally quick. He picked up a large, thick branch from the ground and hit the eagle with it, catching it right on the top of one of its heads.

The eagle fell on to the creeper which wrapped itself around the bird, causing it to drop it's prey. The relieved rabbit promptly bolted.

Meanwhile, Milo delved into one of his bags and found a paper knife which he used to hack at the part of the creeper that still held Jody's ankle.

Three hacks with the knife succeeded in forcing the creeper to release Jody from it's grip and concentrate instead on squeezing harder on the bird.

Milo pulled Jody clear as the giant bird began to fight for its life by pecking and clawing at the plant. But it was to be a fight the bird would lose as the creeper increased the pressure on both of the eagle's swollen necks.

Within seconds the bird was strangled to death. "Thank you so much, Bag ...Milo," Jody stuttered.

Olaf quickly inspected her ankle and wiped it clean. "Does it hurt at all? Can you move it?" he asked.

Jody moved her ankle up and down. "Yes, it's all right." "Fortunately the eagle doesn't appear to have done any damage to you either," said the pixie. "You were very lucky to escape."

Jody smiled at The Bag Man and Olaf sheepishly. "Thank you both so much. You saved my life."

The Bag Man's face creased into a broad grin. "You're very welcome," he said. "That makes us all square, because back in the castle you saved me from a frog's life. But we've got to be careful. If that was one of the witches' eagles then they sent it to attack you."

"But why?" asked Jody, perplexed.

"I'm not sure," replied The Bag Man. "What I do know is that once they discover the secret potion has been destroyed they will be furious. And so will Hugo Toby. We've got to try to get you and your brother to safety as soon as possible."

CHAPTER TWENTY

HUGO TOBY looked out of his horse-drawn carriage as it sped towards his brother's castle.

He peered into the forest and saw three boys with axes in their hands, climbing trees and chopping down branches. Below the boys in the trees, several dogs were barking at three people as they approached them. The three figures were too far away for him to make out their faces, but one of them appeared to be a girl with long golden-brown hair and another seemed to be carrying three bags.

"Surely that can't be the girl I sent to the whirlpool," he said to himself. "But it does look remarkably like her. If she did escape perhaps it was my brother's doing – maybe he rescued her because he wanted her to work for him. But, if not, then she must have been very, very lucky.

"Perhaps I should set her a tougher challenge – like putting her into a barrel of live snakes. I'd like to see if she could escape from that. What do you think, Wham?" He leaned across to stroke his large cat, which was filling the remainder of the carriage seat that was not occupied by his master's bulk.

"It's always good fun to terrorise an aggravating child, isn't it?" Both questions went unanswered by Wham, who was beginning to look forward to another meal of giant prawns. "You're no good when it comes to giving advice, are you, Wham?" Hugo Toby chided. "I'd better refer to my lucky coin instead." He fished in the top pocket of his robe and brought out his special golden coin.

"Now," he said. "If it comes down 'heads' it is the same girl." The wizard tossed the coin in the air, caught it on the palm of his hand and inspected it. It was 'heads'

"And if it comes down 'heads' again she is up to no good." He spun the coin a second time and once more it landed 'heads' up. "That's very interesting," he mused.

Hugo poked his head out of the carriage window and shouted at his driver, a pathetically tall, thin goblin with gigantic ears and a pointed nose. "Faster," he ordered. "We need to go faster."

Finally, the carriage arrived at the castle. The driver, having suffered the indignity of being searched by the two guards outside the front gate, put all Hugo Toby's bags in the hall before leaving without getting a tip or even a 'thank you'.

Hugo, holding his walking stick and a lead attached to the collar of a disgruntled Wham, demanded to see his brother. "I'm sorry sir, but Augustine has gone out," Grog told him. "Where?" insisted Hugo Toby, peering at one of the few people he had come across with a more hideous nose than himself. "Presumably he told you where he was going?"

"I don't know. He...he didn't say," stammered the little pixie, his squint and his chewing habit both becoming more pronounced. "He left so quickly he didn't have time to leave a message."

Hugo Toby rubbed his stubbly beard, bent down to stroke Wham's nose, and looked at the pixie suspiciously. "Doesn't sound like my brother to me," he said. "And when will he be back?"

"I don't know, sir. He didn't say," uttered Grog again, shaking with fear.

"You seem to know very little," Hugo scoffed. "Well, don't just stand there, trembling. Here, take my cat." With that he thrust the lead into the little pixie's hand.

"Show Wham to my room. I trust you have prepared a separate bed for him. Make sure he is comfortable."

"Yes, sir," muttered the little pixie, struggling to hold the lead as Wham pulled on it and swished his tail in the air irritably. "I want to be informed as soon as Augustine returns. Tell me, has he got any children working in the forest for him?" The pixie looked increasingly uneasy, but before he could answer Hugo Toby added threateningly: "And don't tell me you don't know."

"Yes, he has" said Grog.

"How many?"

"Three boys," replied the pixie.

"No girls?" asked Hugo Toby again. "Does he have a girl working for him as well?"

"I don't think so, sir" Grog responded, breathing heavily and squinting wildly.

Mr. Toby glared at him. "While I'm waiting for Augustine to return, I think I'll transport myself to the forest and see just what is going on there. Something doesn't seem quite right to me. Make sure you look after my cat while I'm gone. Feed him some giant prawns."

"I'll get the chef to prepare some, sir. Would that be with or without salad?"

"Are you trying to be funny? Just make sure Wham is served a big portion of fresh prawns. If he is still hungry when I get back I'll turn you into a prawn and feed you to Wham." Grog squinted uncontrollably and almost swallowed his tongue.

CHAPTER TWENTY-ONE

BACK in Bromley, Jody's distraught parents Marjorie and Herbert were experiencing a day they never wanted to relive.

It started just before 8 am. when Marjorie's calls up the stairs to Jody went unanswered. Herbert then strode into his daughter's room to awaken her and was shattered to find she was not there.

He did not go to work and they frantically telephoned the homes of Jody's friends, only to be told she had not been there.

"We must go to the police immediately and report Jody missing," said Marjorie.

"Yes, of course we must," Herbert agreed.

"It's absolutely dreadful," Marjorie continued. "It was bad enough when James disappeared. I thought my heart would break. But for Jody to go missing as well – it's more than I can take."

"Maybe Jody has gone to look for James," suggested Herbert. "No doubt that is what the police will suspect. Unless they think that we are to blame – in which case they will probably give us a grilling."

Small beads of sweat began to gather on Herbert's brow just below his receding hairline as his sub-conscious told him there was something more sinister about James's disappearance.

If only he could remember what it was.

Marjorie's green eyes, which had been shedding tears almost non-stop, now flashed angrily at him. But Herbert was in full flow. "The police might think we are responsible. They could jump to the conclusion that we ill-treated the children and they both ran away from home. Or, even worse, they may accuse us of getting rid of them."

Marjorie looked at her husband with contempt. "How can you be more concerned with what might happen to us than with what has become of Jody?" she stormed, her annoyance causing her cheeks to redden and make her freckles almost unnoticeable.

Herbert, normally full of confidence and assertiveness, dropped his shoulders in shame. "I was only...." he started to bluster but changed his mind. "I'm sorry," he said, sheepishly. "Of course, you are right. Let's go down the police station straight away."

Marjorie, an attractive woman despite her plump figure, was already pulling her full-length coat over her ample frame. "It could be that someone has abducted both our children. But I think it is more likely that, as you said, Jody has gone to look for James."

So Mr. and Mrs. Richards went along to Bromley police station to report their daughter missing to the same two officers who were looking into the disappearance of their son.

This time the policemen were not so understanding and, as Herbert had predicted, they relentlessly fired questions at the couple for nearly two hours.

But Herbert didn't mention anything about what he had found on James's computer disc concerning the Castle of Dreams. He couldn't – he simply had no memory of it.

CHAPTER TWENTY-TWO

THE Bag Man, accompanied by Jody and Olaf, had found the spot in the forest where the boys were working, and had taken care of the original six guard dogs by giving them some more meat covered with sleeping potions.

Even the seventh dog – alias Bodger – succumbed to the pangs of hunger and ate the meat, but the other dog in black boots, Enoch, refused. Instead, Enoch growled ferociously at them, baring his large, dirty teeth.

He moved menacingly towards Jody, hell bent on seeking revenge for her causing Augustine The Awful to turn him from a goblin into a dog. Jody was filled with horror as anger blazed in the dog's eyes.

The Bag Man moved between them, but still the dog came forward. This caused the Bag Man to edge slowly backwards, trying not to let Olaf see the terror he was feeling.

The animal evaded the Bag Man's attempt to grab him and leapt at the girl. Before he could sink his teeth into her, however, he was sent flying by a hefty blow delivered by James, who had raced up and swung the blunt end of his axe at the side of the dog's head.

Enoch yelped in agony and fell to the ground in a heap, dazed.

"Are you all right?" asked James anxiously, catching Jody as she tottered unsteadily.

"Yes, I'm OK – thanks to you," she said. "I didn't think he would be so vicious."

"Perhaps you could take the dog back to the castle," the Bag Man asked Olaf. "Have you got a lead for him?"

"No," said Olaf.

"Then you'll have to use your belt," shouted James. "Yes, Olaf, use your belt as a lead," the Bag Man urged.

The large pixie reluctantly started to remove his belt and immediately his trousers dropped two or three inches, causing him to hoist them up. "Bodger or Enoch should be here with the dogs, I don't know what could have happened to them," he said.

"That dog you are about to put a lead on IS Enoch," Jody told him.

"What!?" exclaimed Olaf.

Enoch was now recovering and he growled fiercely at Olaf, who backed away.

"Yes," said the Bag Man. "Augustine The Awful turned Enoch and Bodger into dogs. Now if you don't want to become a dog, too, perhaps you would be good enough to fasten your belt to Enoch's collar and take him back to the castle." Olaf certainly did not want to run the slightest risk of suffering the same fate as Enoch. So he persevered despite the fact the dog bit him twice.

The snarling beast was about to attack again, but just as Enoch prepared to leap at Olaf he suddenly had a sneezing fit and could only stand spluttering helplessly. The pixie recovered his composure and by the fifth sneeze Olaf had managed to get the belt attached to Enoch's collar.

"Well, done, Olaf," the Bag Man exclaimed, quite relieved. "Make sure you give our friend Enoch a bath in the moat around the castle when you get back. That will literally take his mind off any desire he may have to bite you."

Olaf grunted in agreement. He half led and half dragged an enraged Enoch back to the castle with one hand, while using the other to hold up his trousers.

The Bag Man then told James and the other two boys: "There is no time to lose. We have managed to escape from the castle, but Augustine The Awful's brother Hugo could arrive at any minute. We've come to get you and take you with us."

Jody didn't help matters by informing James's friends, a ginger-haired boy with a crew cut and a jolly-looking plump lad, that she was a very naughty girl and couldn't be trusted. It meant a further lengthy explanation after which the ginger-haired boy was still confused. He stood scratching his crew-cut and sliding his tongue over the braces on his teeth. "Don't worry, Nick-Knack," James told him. "She has to say that stuff about being naughty and untrustworthy because a witch has put a curse on her."

"Nick-Knack?" queried Jody. "That's a very strange name." "His name is Nick and we call him Nick-Knack because he has the knack of nicking himself with the clippers when cutting down the berries from the trees," explained James. Nick-Knack held up three fingers with plasters on them by way of confirmation.

"But what if we do trust you and go with you?" asked Nick-Knack, running his hand through his hair which was so short it stuck up like bristles. "When Augustine The Awful finds out that we've gone he'll come looking for us." "There's not much chance of that now because he's been turned into a frog." Jody reasoned.

"Augustine The Awful is now a frog?" asked the third boy, whose large tummy and round face made him look like a trimmer version of the old comic book character Billy Bunter. "That's right," said an agitated Bag Man. "It's a long story and it would be better if we told you later. I suggest you come with us now."

"What do you think, James?" inquired the Billy Bunter look-alike, not unexpectedly referred to by James and Nick- Knack as 'Bunter'. Despite the warm climate, the boy wore an old brown jumper which pulled across his large stomach and had holes in the sleeves where his protruding elbows had caused the wool to wear away.

"I'm tempted, Bunter," James answered. "But I'm just worried about what Jody said yesterday about her being my sister and taking me home. I don't remember her and I certainly don't remember anything about having a home or any parents."

"Look," shouted Jody, becoming annoyed. "I've risked my life coming to Tamila to try to rescue you.

"If you don't want to come then stay here chopping trees for the rest of your life."

"You're right," said James. "What have I got to lose by coming home with you? It can't be as terrible as this, can it?"

Jody grinned at him. "Not unless father is in a bad mood," she joked. "But getting home might not be an option any more. I have now had to use up the second and last wish that Wiffle, the wizard of kindness, granted me – so I can't just wish us home any more."

"Why did you do that?" asked Bunter. "Why did you use the second wish you had?"

Jody tried not to sound indignant. "Augustine The Awful had transformed the Bag...whoops, sorry, I mean Milo, here, into a frog. So I had to use the wish to reverse the spell and place it on Augustine The Awful instead. Now he's a frog and he's in the moat around the castle where the magical water has made him lose his memory.

"The problem is that Augustine The Awful's notes on his formula for everlasting life are still somewhere in the castle."

"Everlasting life?" Bunter questioned.

"Yes," said the Bag Man impatiently. "He has been trying to create a potion that would enable him to live for ever. You boys have been unwittingly helping Augustine to make the formula by providing him with two of the main ingredients." "So that's why he has had us cutting down so many golden berries and pulling out plant life from the river-bed," said James.

"That's right," confirmed Jody. "We found several barrels of berries and one full of plant life in the castle storeroom being guarded by a grotesque monster. It was the most awful thing I've ever seen – far worse than a dragon.

"The monster had already eaten a witch who tried to steal some of the potion and it was getting ready to eat us, too. But we managed to poison it and tip acid into the barrels. "Unfortunately, we didn't have time to search for Augustine The Awful's notes revealing the exact formula. There's a third potion somewhere."

While she spoke two of the guard dogs began to stir. "Look," urged the Bag Man. "We can't afford to waste any more time talking. Are you coming or not?"

"OK," said James. "You've convinced me. Come on, lads – let's go with them right away before the dogs wake up." The ginger-haired boy was still pondering the situation, which prompted Bunter to tell him: "Come on, Nick-Knack

– chop, chop."

But before they could move they heard the sound of bushes being pushed back.

They looked round to find themselves confronted by the imposing figure of Hugo Toby.

CHAPTER TWENTY-THREE

"WHAT have we here?" bellowed Hugo Toby. "Am I interrupting a meeting?" he glared at them with his piercing eyes and raised his black, bushy eyebrows questioningly. "And what are you doing here little girl?"

Jody knew what she had to tell him. "I am a very naughty girl who cannot be trusted," she said.

"You don't have to tell me – I already know that," Mr. Toby answered, showing the same tendency to sneer as his brother had done. "But you've changed somehow – your nose... it's longer. Perhaps it got bigger because you kept poking it into other people's business?"

He laughed at his own attempted joke and then confided: "I certainly didn't expect to see you again."

"No, I'm sure you didn't," said Jody, staring past his own long, pointed nose into those glaring pools that passed for eyes. "You sent me into a whirlpool to die."

"I was merely trying to help you get to where you wanted to go," chuckled Hugo Toby. "I presume you have found your missing brother. Let me guess – he's this blond lad. Now would you be so good as to explain to me what you are doing here? Why you have stopped these boys working and why my brother's dogs are asleep?

"And perhaps you can also tell me where my brother is? I asked the pixie in the castle and did not get a satisfactory answer. But even if the little fellow had twice as many brains he'd only be a half wit – certainly not on your IQ level, Milo."

"Not even on yours," Milo retorted.

"Very witty," replied Hugo, tersely. "But I've no time for banter and my patience is wearing rather thin. Now can I have some answers?"

There was a brief silence, as the boys looked one to the other and then to Jody, hoping that she could think of some suitable explanations.

It was the Bag Man who spoke. He said: "The dogs are just dozing. Your brother is letting Jody take the boys home because he no longer needs them. His quest to find the secret of eternal life is over."

"Has he found it?" demanded Hugo Toby. "Does it work?"

"I don't know, but he certainly looked transformed when we last saw him," replied the Bag Man.

"In what way?" asked Mr. Toby, rubbing his short, prickly, black beard – a habit Jody had noticed when she first met him. "Does he look younger?"

The Bag Man's mind seemed to go blank so Jody spoke up. "He seemed more lively and was bouncing about like someone half his age."

"Yes," chimed in the Bag Man, picking up on the misinformation Jody had provided without a word of a lie. "Your brother was very excited. He left in a hurry. He didn't say where he was going, but he knows you can use your magic powers to join him if you get tired of waiting for him."

"Perhaps this gentleman's powers don't extend that far," James goaded.

"After all, he doesn't know where his brother is, does he?" added Bunter.

124

"Nonsense," scoffed Hugo Toby. "You only have to ask your sister about how I transported her to the whirlpool to know what I am capable of doing. I personally usually prefer to travel by coach, but I'm willing to give you a demonstration if you wish me to banish you somewhere."

"That won't be necessary," Jody interrupted. "I know to my cost that this gentleman has magic powers." She looked anxiously beyond Mr. Toby as another of the dogs started to show signs of waking up.

Hugo Toby stroked his black beard again. "How do I know that if I transport myself to join my brother it won't be some kind of trap?" he rapped suspiciously.

The Bag Man answered his question with another. "How can it be a trap?" he inquired. "You have the magic powers to transport yourself right next to your brother if you want to, so you must believe you could then return the same way. But if you don't wish to do that then you can simply wait for your brother to return."

"I'm getting tired of waiting," snapped Hugo Toby. "I can't hang around all day. If Augustine has found the secret of eternal life I want it, too. So maybe I'll take your advice and send myself next to my brother. I'll just toss my lucky coin to make sure it's the right thing to do."

Hugo Toby took his golden coin out of his pocket and flipped it high in the air – a little too high as it happened because, instead of falling in the palm of his hand, it hit his thumb and landed in the long pink grass. "Now where's that gone?" he cursed. They all looked in the grass and James was the first to spot it. He picked it up and, with a brief hesitation, he called out "Heads."

"That means I go," said Mr. Toby, snatching the coin out of the boy's hand.

Jody's eyes lit up and she turned away so that Hugo Toby could not see her delight. But her expression soon changed, because the malicious wizard added menacingly: "First, I'll make sure you can't run off. You might be telling me lies – so I'll make certain you don't slip away until I've spoken to my brother."

He clicked his fingers and the three boys, Jody and the Bag Man suddenly found themselves surrounded by a cage with long iron bars.

"Uga Oooo," yelled the Bag Man in anguish. "We're trapped," screeched Nick-Knack.

"Let us out," cried Jody as she and James rattled the bars in vain.

"You'll stay there until I find my brother," Hugo Toby told them.

"But we could starve," protested Bunter.

"That's a risk I'll just have to take," chided Hugo. "And to make absolutely certain you don't escape I'll make you all smell of raw meat. That way the dogs will eat you alive if you get out of the cage."

The wicked wizard clicked his fingers again and suddenly the five captives reeked of uncooked meat.

"You can't leave us like this?" Nick-Knack protested.

"I can and I will," sneered Mr. Toby. "And if I find out from my brother that you have been lying to me then I'll stick barrels full of snakes in the cage with you. In fact, I think, as a precaution, I'll put that spell on you now."

"Please don't," pleaded Nick-Knack. "I hate snakes."

But Hugo clapped his hands and muttered an incantation. "Consider it done," he said. "Barrels of poisonous snakes will be tipped into the cage with you by this time tomorrow unless I return to break the spell. So it is in your own interests that I am safe to return in 24 hours time."

An alarmed and agitated Bunter started to protest: "Don't go....there's something...." But before he could complete the sentence the Bag Man had kicked him in the shins. "What's that you were saying?" asked Hugo Toby, looking at the quivering rotund boy.

Before Bunter could reply, the Bag Man interjected: "He doesn't want you to go and leave us stuck in this cage stinking of meat."

"That's too bad," chuckled Hugo Toby, squeezing his long nose together at the tip to prevent the aroma of the raw meat going into his nostrils. "The smell won't kill you – but the snakes WILL if I don't get back in time.

"Well," he sighed. "I've enjoyed our talk, but I can't spend any more time with you exchanging idle chatter. I'm going to wherever my brother is and discover the secret of eternal life."

He clicked his fingers again and was gone.

CHAPTER TWENTY-FOUR

"WE'RE in a real mess now," said Bunter, ruefully, turning on the Bag Man. "We are locked in a cage in the middle of the forest with no means of escape. And to add to our worries we're going to have loads of poisonous snakes tipped in here with us in 24 hours' time.

"Why didn't you let me stop Mr. Toby from going? Now he'll end up next to his brother in the castle's moat, and Jody has told us that the magical water in the moat will make him lose his memory. So he'll never return."

"It's a chance we have to take," said the Bag Man.

"Yes," James agreed. "By going into the moat and losing his memory Hugo Toby cannot rescue his brother or get his hands on any notes Augustine may have left about the formula for everlasting life. At least this way we have 24 hours to get out of this cage."

"But if by some miracle we do get out the dogs will attack us," pointed out Nick-Knack, as Bodger and one of the other large animals staggered to their feet. Despite being drowsy they immediately picked up the smell of the meat and began to prowl menacingly around the cage.

"This is our punishment for telling Hugo Toby lies," Jody muttered, looking accusingly at the Bag Man.

It is so important to be truthful and honest, both Wiffle and her father had told her.

"I promised my father and Wiffle that I would always tell the truth."

"We didn't tell him lies – we simply misled him," protested the Bag Man. "As a frog, his brother was transformed – and we simply told him his brother looked transformed. Augustine was certainly livelier and was jumping about like someone half his age, just as we said.

"Besides, if we had told Hugo Toby what we did to his brother he would probably have killed us. It's much better that he and Augustine are up to their necks in a moat full of stinking water."

"They couldn't stink more than us," Jody reminded him. "Yes," added Nick-Knack, looking at Bunter. "I didn't think it would be possible, but you now smell worse than you used to do."

"What I don't understand," said the Bag Man, "is why Hugo's lucky coin betrayed him."

"It didn't," James told him. "I called 'heads', but the coin actually landed on the 'tails' side."

"That was clever," agreed the Bag Man.

"But how did you know that 'heads' would send him to the moat?" Nick-Knack queried.

"I didn't for sure," James confessed with a grin. "But I assumed that, as it was his lucky coin, it had always given him the right answers in the past. Therefore, it would provide him with the correct answer again. So when I saw it had come down 'tails' I guessed that Toby must have said to himself that 'tails' would indicate he should NOT go looking for his brother."

"Calling 'heads' completely fooled him."

"You told a lie," chastised Jody. "You may not remember, but you also promised father you would never lie."

"I didn't lie," James grinned. "I just called out the word 'heads' – I never actually claimed the coin landed on the 'heads' side. Like Milo said, it's not lying, it's simply misleading someone who deserved to be misled."

"But how do we get out of this cage?" asked Bunter. "We have only 24 hours to do so otherwise we'll be killed by poisonous snakes. And if we do get out the dogs will attack us."

"Someone is bound to come across us eventually," the Bag Man consoled him. "Then they can go for help." Unfortunately, nobody came near the clearing in the forest and, as the sky began to darken, the five prisoners prepared to spend the night sitting in the cramped cage, with seven dogs barking and yelping madly only a matter of inches away. Bodger, prowling around the cage menacingly in his black boots, was particularly fierce. He twice tried to thrust his head through the bars of the cage in vain attempts to attack the girl who had been responsible for goading Augustine The Awful into transforming him from a goblin into a dog.

A scared Jody moved away quickly. "Bodger is determined to get me," she said.

"Don't worry, he can't reach you in here," the Bag Man comforted her.

"I'm hungry," said Bunter.

"We're all hungry," Nick-Knack chided him.

"Well, I can do something about that," the Bag Man replied. He clicked his fingers and on the floor of the cage at their feet appeared the biggest spread of food and drink imaginable. But this made the dogs bark even louder. "I suppose I had better magic up some food for you, too," the Bag Man told the dogs. He clicked his fingers once more and some meat appeared.

As the Bag Man was about to throw it out of the cage to the dogs, Jody stopped him. "Please put some more sleeping potions on it," she urged.

"I forgot about that," the Bag Man admitted. He went through his carrier bags and eventually found a tube that he squirted on the meat as the dogs yelped impatiently. The boys helped him hurl the meat through the bars of the cage. The greedy animals immediately devoured it, which caused them to fall asleep soon after they had finished eating.

But the dog in the boots had ignored the doctored meat. Instead, he continued to prowl around, his brown eyes blazing with fury, as he looked for a way to get into the cage. "Bodger might have been silly enough to take the sleeping potion the first time, but he's not going to fall for the same trick twice," said Jody as the angry dog bared his teeth and growled threateningly at her.

Bunter had already crammed a large portion of chicken pie into his mouth, but Nick-Knack and James stopped eating their smaller portions of food to question the Bag Man. "If you can perform magic then why didn't you stop that nasty wizard putting us in this cage?" asked Nick-Knack. "And more important, why don't you get us out of the cage now?" pressed James between mouthfuls of turkey.

"I once fell foul of Augustine The Awful and he took away most of my magic powers," explained the Bag Man ruefully. "I can only perform basic magic now such as producing food and drink and making it rain. Those are just elementary spells."

"Can you make it rain anywhere?" Jody asked.

"Yes, I suppose so," the Bag Man acknowledged. "Once I played a joke on Wiffle by causing it to rain on his head while everywhere else around him was dry. He was very angry at first, but we are good friends so he soon forgave me. We have often laughed about it since."

"Well, why don't you make it rain on Wiffle again? If the water only fell on him then he would no doubt realise that it was you doing it."

"What would be the point?" asked Nick-Knack, who was not the brightest of boys. "He would only think it was another of the Bag Man's jokes."

"Milo – not The Bag Man," Milo corrected him.

"Maybe Nick-Knack is right," sighed Jody. "But it might occur to Wiffle that Milo was trying to get a message to him and needed his help. After all, it was Wiffle who told me where I could find Milo – and Wiffle was worried I might land in trouble. Surely, it's worth a try."

Bunter also had reservations. "But even if Wiffle thought it was Milo and that it was a cry for help, he wouldn't know where we are, would he?" Bunter pointed out.

Jody looked to James for support and he nodded his agreement. "Like Jody says, it is worth trying," he insisted. "Milo could use the rain in three short bursts so that it comes down on Wiffle and stops and then comes down twice more – it would be like an SOS signal."

"Well, all right. I'll give it a try," the Bag Man conceded. "But I don't think Wiffle will be too pleased if I make it rain on his head, particularly if he's sitting on his expensive furniture. Besides I don't know whereabouts he is in the house.

"I'll just cause it to rain very hard immediately outside his front door and against his windows. If he doesn't see it he is bound to hear it."

"You should repeat the three bursts several times just to make absolutely sure," urged Bunter, gulping down another pie.

The Bag Man nodded and said: "OK, let's go for it."

He then muttered a few strange words, clicked his thumbs against his fingers quickly and repeated the action four times.

"Now all we can do is wait and hope," he told them with a sigh.

But six hours passed very slowly and there was no sign of Wiffle.

They were consumed with a feeling of despair as they sat down and tried to get through the night huddled together tightly in the middle of the small cage.

CHAPTER TWENTY-FIVE

WHEN the sun began to gain strength the next morning they were all exhausted, having been unable to get much sleep in their confined space.

Jody rubbed her legs where cramp was starting to set into her calf muscles. She noticed that James was also massaging his legs, while Bunter was hopping around in discomfort, obviously needing to go to the toilet after drinking and eating far too much the previous day.

"Good morning," the Bag Man greeted her.

"Good morning, Milo," she replied continuing to try to massage the cramp away. She put one hand on the cage bars as she rubbed with the other hand.

"Look out," shouted the Bag Man.

The warning came too late. Although Jody hastily withdrew her hand she was not quite quick enough. The dog in the black boots made a wild lunge towards her hand and managed to bite one of her fingers before his teeth grated against the metal bars of the cage. It caused Bodger to chip one of his teeth and he howled out in pain.

His cry was partly drowned by that of Jody, who fell to the floor, writhing in agony. "He got me that time," she sobbed, holding her injured finger, which was bleeding profusely. "Let me see," said James, loosening her grip so that he could take a look at the bleeding finger. "That's a very nasty bite – it's so deep it might have gone down to the bone." The Bag Man went across to one of his carrier bags and pulled out a white shirt, from which he tore off a sleeve and started to bind up her finger.

Jody cried out as he pressed the wound together. Although the Bag Man tried to dress her cut gently, she felt as if someone was touching her finger with a hot poker, and a wave of nausea swept over her. Finally the Bag Man had finished and the girl sighed with relief.

She managed to mutter bravely through her sobs: "I just hope it's not infected. But I suppose that's the least of our worries."

"Our attempt at trying to send an SOS signal to Wiffle obviously hasn't worked," reflected Bunter, moving from one foot to the other.

"No. I suppose it was a silly idea," admitted Jody. "It seems we are sunk. There are only a few hours left before this cage is full of poisonous snakes."

"It was worth trying," James comforted her. "Has anyone got any other ideas?" Nobody had.

"In that case I suggest we try the rain trick one more time," James said to Milo. "Perhaps Wiffle didn't even notice the bursts of rain you sent outside his front door."

"They would have made quite a noise," the Bag Man told him.

"But if it was raining already or if Wiffle was listening to music or watching television then he would not have heard the bursts of rain. So let's try it again now.

"You could make it rain just INSIDE Wiffle's front door in the hall as well as OUTSIDE so that he's sure to see it or hear it."

"All right," said the Bag Man. "I'll repeat three more bursts of rain outside his front door and three bursts INSIDE." He muttered a spell and clicked his thumbs against his fingers twice, then did it twice more.

The next few hours seemed an eternity as they stood helplessly in the cage. It was particularly awful for Bunter, who was not completely successful in overcoming his urge to wee, and his trousers became slightly stained.

Jody had problems of her own. Her finger had swollen and the pain increased. Her head ached and she began to break out in a sweat. "I'm feeling rough," she muttered.

"That bite has made her ill," said James. "She needs a doctor. It could be poisonous."

"Soon we're all going to be poisoned by snake bites," Nick-Knack reminded them. "I can't bear to think about having the slimy things near to me."

At that moment a large cloud of green smoke appeared outside the cell and two fearsome figures suddenly emerged from it – Hugo Toby and his brother Augustine! Even their odour exuded evil.

"Uga Oooo," cried the Bag` Man in disbelief.

Jody cowered in fear as Augustine's menacing black eyes sought her out."You obviously didn't expect to see us again," said Hugo harshly. "They don't look pleased to see us, do they Augustine?"

"That's probably the understatement of the year," sneered his brother, moving towards the cage menacingly.

"But how did you get away from the moat?" stammered Buster. "We thought you had been turned into a frog." Hugo smirked. "So he was – and if you had had your way I would have joined him in the moat and lost my memory, too. But fortunately, Augustine had climbed out of the water on to the grassy bank and that's where I landed.

"I must admit that when I saw a frog next to me my first instinct was to kick it back into the moat, but I realised just in time that as I had wished to be next to Augustine he must be the frog. So I changed him back to his old self and restored his memory. I am indebted to you for sending me to him." Augustine The Awful's stare seemed to go straight through Jody, who was sitting in the cage in a dazed state. "Now it is time to settle some old scores," he said, his face full of rage. "The girl and the Bag Man are going to pay dearly for turning me into a frog and throwing me out of my own castle."

"Yes," said Hugo. "They must all suffer because they tried to destroy both of us."

The Bag Man moved to the front of the cage and looked deep into Augustine's eyes. "You can do what you like to me," he said. "But don't hurt these poor children. Jody has been bitten by one of the dogs and is becoming delirious – she needs some medicine urgently."

Augustine stared at the girl, slumped on the floor of the cage. "I'll give her something to make her forget her pain," he said. With that he clicked his fingers and in his hand there appeared a bottle containing some dark and murky looking liquid. He chanted some unintelligible words and the bottle suddenly left his hand to land at Jody's feet. "What is it?" asked Jody, drowsily, her head throbbing and her vision becoming slightly blurred.

"As I said, it will make you forget your pain," Augustine replied. "I want you to be fully focused when I punish you for turning me into a frog."

Jody picked up the bottle, unscrewed the top and raised it to her mouth.

"Don't drink it," warned James.

She hesitated, then heeded his advice and put the bottle down.

"As you wish," Augustine told them. "Enough of this time wasting. The girl and the Bag Man must now suffer for what they did."

Hugo interceded. "May I suggest, dear brother, that I merely bring forward the spell I cast before I left – to fill their cell full of poisonous snakes?"

Augustine's face twisted into an evil smile. "That will do nicely for starters," he said.

Hugo clicked his fingers and suddenly two barrels landed with a tremendous thud on the floor of the cell. They were both full of snakes.

"Oh, no," cried Nick-Knack. "Don't let them near me. I hate them."

"The snakes are already starting to crawl out of the barrels," shouted Bunter, watching in horror as two large, venomous-looking snakes slithered from the open top of one over-full barrel and down the side of it towards the bottom of the cage.

"What can we do?" James asked the Bag Man.

"Snakes are scared of fire," Milo responded. "If I can set fire to the rest of that shirt I tore then we can use it to ward them off."

"But that won't last long, will it?" Bunter protested.

They all moved as far away from the barrels as they could, with their backs pressed against the opposite side of the cage, while Milo fumbled in his bags to find some matches. But the two snakes, fangs exposed, approached to within inches of where Jody was standing, causing her body and arms to shake with fright. The shock of seeing the snakes had made her less drowsy and she now stood on tip-toe in the hope that it would take her further away from the slimly serpents.

Nick-Knack was also overcome with fear. "Get them away from me," he screamed.

The Bag Man lit the shirt and waved it frantically at the snakes just in time to drive them back.

But six more even bigger snakes began to appear, three from each barrel, hissing loudly to show their displeasure. Jody and the boys were terrified.

Augustine and Hugo Toby watched in delight. "This is great entertainment, Hugo," said his brother. "You have excelled yourself."

The shirt burnt brightly for a while. Then it crumbled into a mass of ash. And several snakes moved relentlessly forward, fangs sticking out in expectation as they went in for the kill.

CHAPTER TWENTY-SIX

THE Bag Man frantically pulled off his coat and set that on fire as well. He dangled it in front of the snakes and it had the desired effect by causing them to slither away.

But he admitted: "My coat won't burn for long, either. You boys will have to take some clothes off as well, so that we can use them as torches. Can someone hand me something else?"

"It's hopeless," sighed Nick-Knack.

"Shut up," yelled a frantic Bunter, struggling to pull off his jumper. As he did so he looked up into the clouds, which seemed to be parted by something emerging from them. "What's that?" he exclaimed.

The Bag Man, James and Nick-Knack were too pre-occupied with the snakes, but Jody also peered into the sky. At first she thought she was simply feverish and not focusing properly.

She shielded her eyes from the sun with her hand and stared hard at the object as it drew closer. Even with her vision slightly blurred, she could make out a white flying horse.

"It's Wiffle," she cried with delight. "He's come to rescue us."

"Uga Oooo" exclaimed the Bag Man.

Soon they could clearly see the large, friendly figure of the white-bearded Wiffle, sitting astride his graceful horse Nesbeth. The horse came to rest immediately outside the cage between the six still drowsy dogs.

Augustine and Toby, looking like gunslingers in a wild-west scene, went for their wands, but Wiffle was too quick for them.

"Red hot hands" he cried, clicking his fingers. Immediately the Toby brothers' hands were struck by bolts of flame, and they dropped their wands.

"I don't need a wand to beat you," Augustine The Awful stormed, his voice full of venom. "Statues" he yelled, and raised his hand to weave a spell on his adversary.

But Wiffle was again one move ahead of him and before Augustine could complete the curse, the white-haired wizard waved his sparkling silver wand at the Tobys and said: "Reverse."

With that the Toby brothers became motionless – they were suddenly frozen like statues, having had Augustine's spell reversed on them.

But the danger was not yet over. A furious Bodger ran up and barked fiercely at Wiffle. The dog circled around Nesbeth menacingly, causing the startled horse to rear up. Wiffle remained calm, however, and snapped his fingers to make the dog stop in his tracks. Bodger tried desperately to move, but it was as if an invisible lead was holding him back.

"Oh, Wiffle," Jody called to him weakly. "I'm so glad you came."

"Yes," added the Bag Man. "We couldn't be more delighted to see you. Can you please get rid of these snakes?" As he spoke the snakes slithered forward again, hissing fiercely. "Consider it done," said Wiffle, snapping his fingers once more. Immediately the barrels and the snakes disappeared. But, as the boys jumped about with joy, Jody suddenly let out an agonising cry. "Oh, no" she shrieked at the top of her voice.

"What's the matter?" James asked, concerned. "Is that dog bite getting worse?

"It's not that," she wailed. "I forgot about the curse the witch had placed on me. I didn't tell Wiffle I was a very naughty girl who couldn't be trusted and now my nose has grown another half inch."

They all looked at her nose, which she had covered with her hands. When she took them away it was enormous.

"Well, let me start by putting that right and making the dog bite better, too," boomed Wiffle so that the traumatised girl could hear him through her sobs.

He clapped his hands with the result that Jody's nose was instantly restored to its right size and her finger was no longer cut.

Her fever was also gone. She was overcome with happiness and relief, but she kept touching her nose to make certain it really was back to normal.

"If you explain what the curse was that the witch placed on you I'll be able to lift it completely," Wiffle added, alighting from Nesbeth, who folded his wings to his body. "But tell me what is that awful smell?"

Jody explained about the spells Hugo Toby had placed on them, first by making them smell of raw meat and then filling their cage with poisonous snakes. And she also told Wiffle what the witch had said; including what would happen if she jumped off a wall again.

Wiffle clapped his hands three times, muttering some magic chant with each clap.

"The curses have been lifted," he said.

"Thank goodness for that," Nick-Knack sighed. "That smell of meat was awful."

"Now let me remove this cage," said Wiffle. As the larger-than-life wizard spoke he clicked his fingers and the cage disappeared.

Immediately, Bunter raced off behind some bushes to relieve himself.

At the same time Bodger, having been straining to break free from the trance Wiffle had put him in, finally did so and leapt forward to attack Jody.

But Wiffle came to the rescue once more. He clapped his hands and the dog was jerked back fiercely as he found himself chained to a nearby tree.

"Thank you Wiffle," muttered a shaken Jody, who knew how close she had come to being savaged by a dog hell bent on revenge.

"He won't harm you now," Wiffle assured her. Bunter returned and exclaimed: "I'm so relieved." "Don't be coarse, Bunter," said James. "I mean relieved that we're all safe at last." Bunter retorted. "You obviously received our latest SOS message and worked it out," the Bag Man said to Wiffle.

"Actually, it was received by someone else," Wiffle replied. "I had a visit from my next door neighbour Mrs. Parker-Smythe this morning to complain about one of my cats having left another deposit on her lawn. It was she who got your message."

"What do you mean?" the Bag Man asked.

"Well, Mrs. Parker-Smythe had just knocked at my front door and had scarcely uttered a few words when three short bursts of rain fell on her head," replied Wiffle.

"Oh, I'm so very sorry," the Bag Man said. "I had no idea something like that would happen."

"It wouldn't have been so bad," Wiffle told him. "But I asked her to step inside the hall and when she did so the three short bursts of water were repeated – the good lady was drenched from head to toe."

The recently caged fivesome lowered their heads in shame. It was a few seconds before they looked up to see that Wiffle's big bushy eyebrows were rising as his face creased into a huge grin. "Actually it was quite hilarious," he assured them. "It was all I could do to prevent myself laughing until after she had gone. Unfortunately, to make matters worse, my parrot chose that moment to cry out some of the words Mrs. Parker-Smythe had used when she met Jody." "Which words were they?" Jody asked.

"First he treated her to 'Fancy getting your hair wet through – you silly girl' and then he reminded her that 'Ladies don't have accidents'."

They all fell about laughing and Jody was almost doubled in two with hysterics. "Poor Mrs. Parker-Smythe," she said in mock sympathy.

The Bag Man finally returned to more serious matters. "Presumably, you guessed that the rain showers were caused by me," he said.

Yes," Wiffle replied. "I remembered it was a repeat of the joke you once played on me. But this time I thought it might be serious. Even you wouldn't have dared to play such a silly trick twice."

"We did send bursts of water outside your front door yesterday as well, but perhaps you didn't hear them," said James.

"No, I was out a lot of the time," Wiffle informed him. "But when I returned I found my doorstep was very wet."

"How did you know where we were?" chimed in Bunter.

"I didn't for sure," admitted Wiffle. "But I had meant to check up on Jody anyway. As she had not returned I feared she might have got into some difficulties, even though she didn't summons my little fairy on the magic whistle Heatherbelle had given her." Jody looked guilty. "I'm afraid I lost the whistle when I jumped over a wall and landed on the witch."

"Never mind," said Wiffle. "Milo's rain trick reminded me that I had told Jody about him. So I decided the least I could do was to fly over to the Island of Visions myself and look for you. I had an inkling you might be near Augustine The Awful's castle.

"What was it like to meet up with your old enemy Augustine again, Milo? Not very nice, I should imagine."

"To quote Augustine himself, that would be the understatement of the year," reflected the Bag Man.

"You must tell me all about it," Wiffle replied.

Jody and the Bag Man explained to the wizard in detail about their capture and escape.

"Well, well, well," mused Wiffle. "I'd have loved to have seen Augustine Toby turned into a frog. Unfortunately, he is now back to normal and as soon as my spell wears off he and his brother will revert to their old evil ways."

"How long will the spell you've put on them last?" asked Jody, looking across at the statuesque figures of the Toby brothers.

"Not long," sighed Wiffle. "Then they'll be back to wreck havoc as they look for the secret of everlasting life." At that very moment Augustine The Awful's enormous mental strength enabled him to finally free himself from the spell.

Both he and Wiffle went for their wands, but this time the evil wizard was a fraction quicker and his cry of "Red hot hands" caused Wiffle to drop his silver stick.

Augustine was in his element and was in the middle of uttering a curse when Jody acted.

She picked up the bottle Augustine had given her earlier and threw the contents over both him and his brother, who was also slowly regaining movement as Wiffle's earlier spell wore off. Their heads were covered in dirty water, which ran down their faces. No more words came from Augustine's rubbery lips. Instead, he seemed completely bemused. Hugo appeared equally puzzled.

Augustine and Hugo looked at each other and then at Wiffle, Jody and The Bag Man without any hint of recognition. "What's going on?" demanded Augustine? Do I know any of you?"

"Don't you remember?" asked Bunter.

"If I did I wouldn't be asking you, would I?" Augustine replied, spitefully.

"I can't remember, either," said Hugo, looking equally perplexed.

"Do you mean you've lost your memory?" asked Nick-Knack. "Perhaps I can be of help to you." But before he could say anything more James kicked him on the shin. "Ouch," cried Nick-Knack. "That really hurt."

"Allow me," interjected The Bag Man. "You work in that castle over there." He pointed through the trees to Augustine's castle.

"Why don't you go there now and seek out the pixie called Olaf who is in charge."

Augustine and Toby exchanged bewildered glances. "I work for a pixie?" thundered Augustine.

"You would be wise to show Olaf great respect, especially as you have lost your memory," said The Bag Man. "Why not go to the castle now and speak to him yourself." "Rest assured we will," said Hugo.

With that, they turned on their heels and headed for the castle.

"Well, that's got rid of them," said Jody. "The contents of that bottle must have been water from Augustine's moat so it has caused them to lose their memories. That's why he wanted me to drink it. I'm so glad I didn't."

"You were brilliant," said James proudly.

"Yes," added Wiffle. "Augustine The Awful had disarmed me, but you acted so quickly he didn't have time to put a curse on me. It couldn't have turned out better. Now they have not only forgotten about gaining revenge – they no longer have any memory about wanting to find the secret of everlasting life, either."

"But what about the witches?" asked a bemused Nick-Knack, scratching his crew cut. "There's nothing to stop the witches stealing the golden berry juice and mixing it with their own potions."

"He's right," Bunter told Wiffle. "One witch has already got into the castle's storeroom, only to be eaten by a monster who was guarding the barrels containing some of the special ingredients for the formula. But Jody and the Bag Man poisoned the monster and, as Augustine The Awful has lost his memory, nobody can stop the witches now." Jody, showing a trace of impatience, retorted: "I told you we put acid in each of the barrels. It's strong stuff that burns the rust off cars. If the witches tried to drink that they would be violently sick and I'm sure it would mess up the formula." The Bag Man added: "And the monster wasn't dead. He's probably recovered by now and is still guarding the storeroom. But, as Jody says, the berry juice and plant life in the barrels is ruined anyway."

"That maybe, but Bunter's got a point," argued James. "The witches could still get their hands on Augustine The Awful's notes about the formula."

"Yes, that's true," Jody admitted, pushing a few strands of her wayward hair away from her eyes. "Augustine The Awful told me he had kept notes, but I don't know where." "Don't worry," Wiffle assured her. He took from his pocket a voice box and spoke into it. "Heatherbelle, this is Wiffle," he said. "I want you to fly to Augustine The Awful's castle right away and search for the notes he has left, naming the ingredients for his formula for everlasting life. Make sure that neither Augustine nor his brother, Hugo see you. When you find the notes you are to destroy them.

"Can you also inform a pixie in the castle called Olaf that Augustine and Hugo now believe Olaf is their master because they have lost their memories. Advise him that it would be best to keep it that way.

"You had better tell Olaf as soon as you get there because Augustine and Hugo are on their way to the castle now. Thank you, Heatherbelle. Good-bye."

"That's great," said Jody. "Not only can Heatherbelle hear the whistle, but you can talk to her, too, through your voice box."

"Yeah, that's really neat," Bunter remarked sarcastically. "We have something just like that, though. We call it a mobile phone." He couldn't help smirking.

Wiffle gave Bunter a scornful look. "There is a big difference between this and a mobile phone," he said. "The person I contact has no receiver – they just automatically hear my voice."

"What about Bodger?" asked James, looking over to the dog, which was yelping and trying frantically to free himself from being tied to the tree.

"Ah, Bodger," reflected The Bag Man. "What shall we do with him?"

Wiffle replied: "I think we had better send him for a dip in the moat around the castle. It will clear his mind completely of all those wicked thoughts." The wizard clicked his fingers twice and Bodger disappeared. "That was a great idea," Jody told him. "But James and these other two boys have lost their memories, too. James can't recall anything of his life back in England."

"In that case let me restore their memories," said Wiffle. He clapped his hands, muttered a few strange words, and James immediately recognised Jody as his sister. "Jody, I'm so sorry I didn't remember you," James apologised, putting his arms around her and hugging her.

"That wasn't your fault," the delighted girl assured him. "Augustine The Awful took your memory away to ensure you would stay and work for him. Even if he hadn't I wouldn't have blamed you for not recognising me with the long nose the witch had given me." "I know I can be a bit thick sometimes," said Nick-Knack, scratching his spiky hair. "But what I can't understand, is why Augustine The Awful needed us at all.

"Why didn't he just use his magic powers to get all the golden berries and the river plant life? Surely, he could have just made a series of spells to get them. "

"That's a very good question," Wiffle told him. "I presume Augustine The Awful realised that the Confederation of Wizards were checking up on him and the witches might be spying on him.

"Spells can be traced and he dare not risk doing anything that might lead to others finding out about the ingredients. Who would suspect boys of unwittingly helping to provide a magic potion when on the face of it all they were doing was climbing trees and swimming in the river – things that most boys do?"

"Yes" added the Bag Man. "And the boys were doing all the hard work while Augustine just relaxed."

Nick-Knack still looked puzzled. "But would it have been so terrible if he had discovered the secret of everlasting life?" he asked.

"Yes it would," replied Jody. "He told me he would have more time to increase his riches and his power until he could rule the world."

"Well," James sighed. "That's all very interesting, but we still have one problem now – how are we going to get home?" The children looked towards Wiffle appealingly.

"Unfortunately, I can't send you back to the real world," the white-haired wizard sighed.

CHAPTER TWENTY-SEVEN

"WHY can't you send us back?" Bunter demanded.

Wiffle disregarded the boy's abrupt manner and answered the question calmly. "As some evil wizards like Augustine The Awful were abusing the rules of the Confederation of Wizards, it has been decreed that every member of the Confederation has to abide by a strict code of conduct.

"I won't bore you with all the details, but part of the code of conduct restricts us to granting only two wishes to visitors during any one time zone. Unfortunately, Jody has used both of those wishes I was empowered to grant."

"I don't understand," a confused James told him. "Why do you need to grant us wishes? Can't you just use your magic powers to transport us all home?"

"I'm afraid not," explained Wiffle. "To transport someone from the real world to Tamila or back again on a permanent basis has to be done in the form of a wish. That is why Augustine The Awful had to make sure you three boys would wish to come to Tamila by first convincing you what a wonderful time you could have here."

"But what about me?" pressed Jody. "Augustine The Awful didn't influence me."

"He didn't need to," Wiffle told her. "You were so anxious to follow James that you came to Tamila in a dream. You have been able to stay here because you wished to remain and I granted that wish."

Jody's expectant look was replaced with one of despair. "So we'll never we able to return home," she said, dropping her shoulders in dejection.

"All is not lost," Wiffle said, smiling as he patted the remaining six dogs, which had gathered obediently at his feet. "It is still possible for you to return home within the rules of the Confederation of Wizards."

"I don't understand," said Nick-Knack.. "Can you explain?" Jody asked Wiffle. "Well, as you know, I have just returned from the Wizards' Convention so I learned all the latest developments about rules and amendments. For example, as I just told you, the rules concerning each wizard granting wishes were changed to two per time zone. And a time zone is a period of three months."

"That means we must stay here another three months, I suppose," James surmised.

"Not necessarily," Wiffle corrected him. "You see, another wizard could grant you three young people another two wishes."

"And do you know a wizard who would do that for us?" Bunter asked.

"I do indeed," replied Wiffle, a board smile returning to his face. "You need look no further than Milo.

"You see, the Convention listened to how he had been relieved of most of his magic powers by Augustine The Awful and, by a unanimous vote, it was decided to restore them."

He turned to The Bag Man. "So, Milo, I have been entrusted with the task of making you a fully fledged wizard."

With that, he clapped his hands, placed each of them upon Milo's shoulders and muttered an incantation that was barely audible. Then he announced: "It's done!" and hugged Milo by way of congratulations.

"That's fantastic," uttered the Bag Man. "It means I can now practice my craft again. And I can start by granting you children two wishes. Obviously you want to use the first one to return home.

"That's right," they chorused.

The Bag Man rummaged through his carrier bags. "Let me just check in my book on 'Spells And How To Use Them' to refresh my memory on what I need to do," he announced. While he was looking Wiffle spoke to the children. "May I suggest how you use the second wish," he said, more by way of a statement than a question.

"How?" Jody asked.

"Well," Wiffle responded. "If you just turn up at home you will all have a lot of explaining to do to your parents.

"You, Jody, will have been missed by now – you've been gone three days. Also the boys will have to tell their parents, their schools – and the police – why they have been missing so long, and I doubt if anyone will believe them."

"That's true," commented Nick-Knack. "I hadn't thought of that."

"Yes," added Jody with a frown. "The police have spoken to my parents about James several times. The last time they came round to our house they seemed very suspicious. My father insisted James had been kidnapped, but the police thought he might have run off because I had told them he had spoken to me about wanting to go on an adventure holiday. There's been a massive search for him."

"So what are you suggesting?" asked Bunter.

Wiffle smiled patiently and continued: "I propose that you wish for Milo to take you all back in time to how your home life was before you three boys were snatched by Augustine The Awful. Then nobody will ever know you went missing and your lives can continue as normal."

"That sounds a great idea to me," Jody remarked. "But won't the police remember that they searched for James?" "No," replied Wiffle firmly. "By going back almost four weeks in time it means nothing will have happened. As far as everyone in England is concerned you children will never have been away."

"Perfect – just perfect," James agreed. "That way I won't be expected to study like mad to make up for all the time I've been off school." They all laughed.

Milo finally found his battered old book and pulled it triumphantly out of one of his carrier bags. "Now let me read up on how to grant you two wishes," he said. He flicked through the pages and began to read.

"Why don't you use briefcases instead of the carrier bags?" James inquired.

"I used to," Milo informed him. "But they became so full of my old papers and books that I needed somewhere else to put the new papers and books. Carrier bags are so much more flexible. Now I've found out how to do the spell so I'm all set."

He uttered a spell from his book and told them: "You can now have two wishes and they will be granted."

"That means it is time to say good-bye to you and to Tamila," Jody sighed. "Can we ever return to see you both?"

"Yes, you can come here for a brief visit in your dreams," Wiffle assured her.

"We'd love to see you again," added Milo.

"Thank you – we owe you both so much," Jody told them. "You have both been so kind to us."

The boys said their 'thank yous' as well and took it in turns to shake hands with Wiffle and Milo.

But Jody outdid them by adding: "Whatever we say we can never thank you enough." She then went up to Milo and Wiffle and planted a big kiss on each of them.

"Uga Oooo," cried the Bag Man. "That will do nicely. In fact, you have earned the right to go down in the book in red ink." "Does that wipe out all the black marks you've given me?" Jody suggested, smiling.

"I suppose it does," the Bag Man acknowledged. "Anyway, we are very grateful," added James.

"Just be good children – that will be thanks enough," Wiffle grinned. "And if you do remember anything of your adventures in Tamila you must resist the temptation to tell people about them because Milo is sending you back four weeks in time.

"But I think it is unlikely that you will have any recollection of your adventures with us.

"To make sure things are back to normal I may ask Heatherbelle to come and see how you are getting on. And if you are being good children."

"We'll do our best to be good," Jody assured him. "Now I suppose I had better make my two wishes.

"I wish that we are all back in our homes and everything is as it was before the boys disappeared."

There was a sudden flash of brilliant light and they were no longer in Tamila!

CHAPTER TWENTY-EIGHT

"JODY," the cry was almost deafening. It was her father's voice. "Will you wake up!" he yelled up the stairs to her. "Otherwise you'll be late for school."

Jody opened her eyes to find herself staring at blue and white striped wallpaper. She was back home in her bedroom. "Can you hear me, Jody?" her father called again.

She climbed out of bed and ran to the top of the stairs in her pink pyjamas.

"Are you calling me, Dad?" she asked, unnecessarily, in her confused state.

"Of course I'm calling you," her father bellowed. "Now for goodness sake get ready. Your school holiday is over and you've got to go back today. Why didn't you come down when your mother called you earlier?"

"Sorry," Jody mumbled. And then added, without even thinking, "I am a very naughty girl who cannot be trusted." Her father mellowed. "There's no need for you to exaggerate," he said in a more affectionate tone. "Let's just say you are a bit thoughtless at times."

"Thank you, Dad," she replied, gratefully. "I'll get ready." But her joy at being home suddenly turned to cold fear. Why had her father not called James as well? Obviously her brother had not returned with her despite the wishes she made to the Bag Man. Was James still in Tamila? "Where's James?" she cried out in panic. "What's happened to him?"

Her mother appeared at the foot of the stairs. "Nothing has happened to him," she said, puzzled by the concern in her daughter's voice. "He's still in bed asleep, dear."

"But if he is, why didn't Daddy call him as well?" asked Jody. "Why do you, think, stupid?" a familiar voice chided behind her.

She turned to see James, dressed in dark blue pyjamas, stagger out of his bedroom, wiping the sleep from his eyes. "It's because my school goes back a day later than yours," he told her.

"I didn't have to get up early today and was planning on having a lie-in, but I couldn't sleep with all the racket you're making."

Then he called out to his mother: "Mum, I've had the most peculiar dream."

HOW TO OBTAIN MORE FANTASY NEWS - AND BOOKS AT REDUCED PRICES

To hear all the latest news about Jody Richards and other fantasy adventure books, contact Fantasy Adventure Books by visiting the website: **www.fantasyadventurebooks.com**

There is something for children of all ages, including Heather Flood's books for younger children, **Mousey Mousey and the Witches' Spells**, **Mousey Mousey and the Witches' Revenge** and **Giant Sticker Monster and Other Children's Stories**.

Heather's wonderful books have been compared by reviewers to Julia Donaldson, Enid Blyton and Beatrix Potter.

To obtain signed copies at discounted prices just visit **www.fantasyadventurebooks.com**

These books are also available as both e-versions and paperbacks on Amazon.

TONY FLOOD'S CELEBRITY BOOK FOR ADULTS

Tony Flood has interviewed a galaxy of big name stars from the worlds of show business and sport during his career as a journalist and Controller of Information at Sky Television. He has written a 'tell all' celebrity book called **My Life With The Stars** in which there are revelations and amusing anecdotes on Frank Sinatra, Joan Collins, Paul McCartney, Patsy Kensit, Elvis Presley, Bruce Forsyth, Muhammad Ali, George Best and a host of others.

For details and to obtain a signed copy at a special discounted price visit the website:
www.celebritiesconfessions.com

My Life With The Stars is also available on Amazon.

48618123R00096

Printed in Poland
by Amazon Fulfillment
Poland Sp. z o.o., Wrocław